MYSTERY OF THE EGYPTIAN MUMMY

SCOTT PETERS

BEST DAY BOOKS
FOR YOUNG READERS

Author Scott Peters

Cover design © S.P. Wyshynski
ISBN-13: 978-0-9859852-9-5
ISBN-10: 0-9859852-9-1

Best Day Books For Young Readers

CHAPTER 1

THE MUMMY

"*OOOooooooooooo . . .*"

The ghostly moan filled the night air.

Twelve-year-old Zet bolted upright on his sleeping mat. What was that strange noise?

"*OOOooooooooooo . . .*"

There it came again, like a man in groaning agony. Where was it coming from?

From overhead the yellow moon god, Khonsu, peered down. Sweat stood out on Zet's forehead. He and his eleven-year-old sister Kat were camped out on the rooftop to try and escape the heat. They disagreed on a lot of things—but when it came to keeping cool at night, they were united. The roof was their domain.

Zet spun to check on Kat. Her sleeping pallet lay on the roof's far side.

He gasped. It was empty.

"Kat?" he whispered.

No answer.

By the gods, where was she?

"*OOOooooooooooo . . .*"

The moan sounded close. Creepy close. But that was impossible.

How would a moaning man get up here? Zet leaped to his feet. Where was his sister?

He clambered down the steep ladder to the front room.

"Kat?" he whisper-shouted.

He found her clinging to their mother. The two of them were staring out the open front door. His sister's shoulders were scrunched around her ears in terror.

Still, she shot him a reproachful glance and hissed, *"Shush!"*

Good old Kat.

"What's out there?" Zet demanded, trying to see past them.

"Stay back," his mother said, blocking the door. "Both of you."

"Let me see," he said, standing on tiptoe.

From outside, fresh moans made Zet's short hair prickle. He pushed forward. "Mother, let me see!"

Kat elbowed her brother as Zet gained a foothold in the doorway.

"It's not safe!" his mother cried. "Close the door. Quickly!"

But Zet was already on the front stoop.

The moon painted their street in shades of grey and blue. The eerie colors only heightened the terror that shot through him when he saw the monster.

A bandaged figure.

It looked as horrifying as the ancient stories described: a creature of death come to life. And it was making its way along their street.

The man—or what had once been a man when he'd been alive—was entirely wrapped in tattered cloth strips. His head. His arms. His torso. His legs.

The creepy figure walked with jerky motions. Slow and monotonous, arms outstretched. Ready to throttle any human in its path.

"A mummy," Zet whispered.

His worst dream had come to life, right here in front of his house. A body risen from the dead. How had this mummy escaped its tomb to wander the land of the living? How was that even possible?

What evil had been cast upon it to keep it from eternal peace?

As if sensing Zet's presence, the mummy paused, its face shadowed in darkness. It raised one bandaged arm and pointed a bony finger at Zet. An eerie whisper issued from the mummy's bandaged mouth. A horrible chant.

Awoahaoh huhshhhhh ooohamamima awoahaoh huhshhhhh.

Zet gulped in terror.

Get a hold of yourself! Mummies don't come to life!

Awoahaoh huhshhhhh ooohamamima awoahaoh huhshhhhh.

Was this some kind of joke?

Up and down the street, oil lamps were being lit. The blood-drained faces of horror-stricken neighbors stared at the bandaged creature from windows and doorways. Worried eyes darted from Zet to the mummy and back again.

The mummy kept up its harsh chant.

Finally, it fell silent. Then the mummy resumed its jerking walk.

Without thinking, Zet launched himself toward the street. An enormous jackal, the largest he'd ever seen, leaped from the shadows. Tall, pointed ears jutted from a sleek head and dark, golden fur covered its muscled body. Snarling, it bared its gnashing fangs.

Zet jerked back.

Drool dripped from the animal's jaws. It began to bark, vicious and fast and loud.

It was as if Anubis himself, the jackal-headed God of the Under-world, had come to life in his earthly form and was preparing to launch up their front steps.

Zet edged backward. Every part of him wanted to bolt the door shut. But a small voice inside argued that none of this could be real. It just couldn't. That jackal wasn't a god. And mummies didn't come to life. He needed to find out who or what was behind this. He refused to let this trickery terrorize his family.

The mummy kept on its slow pace down the street.

Zet had to go after it. He needed to see where it was going. The wild beast, however, barred his way. The jackal gnashed its jaws.

Kat's trembling voice cried it, "It's Anubis, come to protect the dead."

The jackal's eyes gleamed. Then it turned and loped after the mummy.

Zet launched after them. Before his feet could hit the street, a hand caught his arm. His mother's.

"Oh no you don't," she commanded.

"Mother, let go!"

"Not even if the gods command it."

"But it's getting away!" he pleaded as the mummy neared the street corner. "Look!"

At that moment, the creature's spooky profile became visible.

Zet choked back a strangled cry. Under the yellow moon, the linen wrappings that covered the monster's face glistened oily black. They were tattered and scorched as though his head had been burned. Where the eyes should have been lay two gaping holes.

Zet's stomach roiled. Kat let out a sharp gasp.

Their mother's arms wrapped tighter around them both, pulling them against her as if to ward off the creature.

From the distant corner, the mummy seemed to glare straight at Zet. It remained frozen, locked in an awful stare.

And then it walked on, moving in its jerky fashion.

The jackal let out a gruesome howl. *Aooooooooh!*

A moment later, the two spooky figures disappeared from view.

Silence reigned for a long, terrible moment. Whispers rose as the neighborhood stirred to life. Across the street, the old sandal-maker hobbled outside. Others joined him.

The sandal-maker pointed a gnarled finger at Zet. "The boy's cursed!" he crowed. "The boy and his family. Cursed!"

The others stared, open-mouthed, at Zet, Kat, and his mother. And it wasn't a good stare. He read fear in their eyes. Not just fear of the mummy, but fear of them.

"We're not," Zet scoffed. "No, we're not!"

The sandal-maker said, "We all saw it point at you. We all heard it whisper that awful curse."

"It wasn't a curse. It was just mumbling!"

The sandal-maker looked ready to argue when a scream pierced the night.

It came from somewhere down the street—a woman's scream. The horrific scream was so loud and awful that Kat clapped her hands over her ears.

The sandal-maker and the other neighbors turned their backs on Zet and ran toward the frightening cries. Zet broke free from his mother and sprinted after them.

Frantic, the crowd scoured the streets for the shrieking woman but her cries had died away.

Despite turning the neighborhood upside down, she was nowhere to be found.

CHAPTER 2
DAYLIGHT FRIGHT

The sun god, Ra, inched his fingers across the rooftop in rosy hues. All night, Zet had lain on his sleeping pallet, eyes wide, replaying the memory of the mummy lurching its way down his street.

It couldn't be real. It just couldn't!

A mummy?

Come back from the dead?

How? Priests had clearly wrapped it in the bandages of eternity. They'd entombed the body. So how had it gotten loose?

Zet was as god-fearing as any Egyptian in Thebes, yet such things didn't happen. Walking mummies belonged in scary stories, whispered over lamplight to frighten your friends and kid sister.

Stories were different. They were fun.

There was nothing fun about last night.

And what were those evil words it had chanted?

Zet rubbed his face. He might be a kid, but he'd made a promise to his father to keep his family safe until the war was over and his father returned. Zet and Kat both had. Together, the siblings worked hard to keep the family's pottery stall running in the marketplace. Their mother and their new baby brother were finally growing stronger, but Zet and Kat couldn't let down their guard.

And now this had happened?

What if the mummy came back? He had to keep that monster away. Even if it meant fighting the creature of death barehanded.

. . . if it *was* a creature of death.

In the light of day, he was finding it hard to believe it was anything more than an awful trick. But who would do such a thing? And why?

He'd get to the bottom of this mystery. Starting now.

He found Kat in the kitchen. She stood lost in thought, a half-peeled orange in one hand. Zet snagged it from her and she started.

"Hey!" she said, "I was about to eat that."

"This month or next? Listen, we need to talk."

She eyed him warily and grabbed another orange from the dish. "Why do I have a bad feeling about this?"

"You know exactly what we have to do."

"No, I don't."

"We're going to investigate, sis."

"Are you crazy? No way," she said. "Not this time—*no way!*"

"Look, come on. That mummy couldn't have been real. We both know mummies don't come back from the dead. They don't walk around in the land of the living. Someone's playing an evil prank. We need to find out why."

"It was no prank. I saw it. That monster's face was half burned off."

"Yeah . . . well." Uneasily, Zet recalled how the monster had stared at him from that singed mask of tattered linen.

"And what about that huge jackal?" Kat demanded.

In the next room, their baby brother Apu wailed. Their mother made cooing noises, trying to settle him.

Kat stepped closer and spoke in a whisper. "Remember Aziza?"

"Aziza?" Zet frowned. "You mean that cousin of Pharaoh?"

"Shh! Yes, of course I mean that cousin of Pharaoh. Who else would I be talking about?"

7

"Well then, yeah."

Aziza's house was the largest in the neighborhood. Back when Aziza had been alive, the man had bullied everyone. He'd talked behind people's backs. Complained about even the smallest noise. And he'd hated kids.

"Aziza was mummified," Kat whispered.

"So?"

"Only because he could afford it," she said in a low voice. "And because he was Pharaoh's cousin."

"Distant cousin. But still related. A fact he never got tired of reminding people. But yes, he was mummified. What's your point?"

Bending closer she said, "Do you think *Aziza* could have come back to haunt us?" Worry pinched Kat's dark brows. "You know . . . for what happened?"

"Don't be silly," Zet scoffed, warding off a shiver. He grabbed a date bun and took a huge bite.

"*Silly?*" Kat glared at him.

Their mother's graceful shadow fell across the doorway. Little Apu sat on her hip, sucking his thumb and looking from Zet to Kat with watery, earnest eyes. His face was red from bawling.

"What's all this whispering?" their mother said.

"Whispering?" Zet said. "We weren't whispering."

Kat quickly said, "Just getting ready to leave for the pottery stall."

"Speaking of which, we better go." Zet reached for the linen-wrapped bowl his mother always prepared with his lunch. "Don't want to be late!"

Their mother eyed the rising sun through the window. It struck Zet that she looked fearful. He could see from the dusky shadows beneath her eyes that she hadn't slept. When she spoke, her voice was strained. "Wait a moment. I want to speak with you, children."

She set Apu on his woven mat. He let out a howl.

"What's got into you, little one?" she asked, sticking a wooden rattle in his chubby fist. "You're usually such a happy monkey."

It was true, Apu was always grinning his drooly grin. But strangely,

Apu had cried all night. Zet and Kat exchanged a glance. *Had the mummy's apparition affected him somehow?*

"I suppose it's growing pains." Their mother watched Apu hammer his rattle against the floor. Then she raised her worried gaze to Zet and Kat. "You're to come right home after closing time. Understand? No loitering around town."

Kat said, "We will."

"Are you two all right?" she asked, reaching to place a cool, soothing hand on their shoulders.

It would be easy for Zet to act like a little kid again. Back when mother made everything better. When he could hide behind her linen skirts from the scary world outside. Yet that boy had disappeared when his father went to war.

He cracked a smile. "Someone's just playing a trick."

"A *trick*?" Kat said. "Stop saying that! The mummy had no face! It's come back from the dead, it's a cursed thing, an unholy thing, and it was in our street. In front of our house. Right out there."

"Shush, you'll scare Apu," Mother said.

Apu threw the rattle and it bounced across the floor.

"Apu has no idea what we're talking about." Zet picked him up and spun him around. Kat darted out of their way. He wheeled his brother around until Apu's wails turned into hiccups and then a reluctant grin. Setting him down, Zet said. "I wish you'd let me go after that mummy last night."

"*Zet*," their mother cautioned.

"At least then we'd know where it went."

"That's for the medjay police to find out," she said.

"Or the priests," Kat said. "Some poor, cursed soul has left his tomb. And he's found his way here. They need to put him back in his sarcophagus. Fast."

"Yes, and they will," their mother said. "They'll sort it out." She shot Zet a stern look. "Without *your* help."

"Who said anything about me helping?"

"You think I don't know my own son?"

"I only want to protect us."

"You'll protect us by doing what you and Kat have already been doing so well. Watching over the pottery stall. Making sales. Keeping the business going while I've been ill." Still holding Kat in one arm, she pulled Zet close. "I don't thank you two enough. You've kept this family alive. Your father will be so proud when he comes home. I'm proud. Promise me you won't get involved in this mummy business."

Zet shuffled his feet. How could he make such a promise?

"Zet?" she asked.

"I'll take care of the stall, don't worry." At least that was true. As to the rest . . .

"Thank you," she said.

Guilt slid over him. Clearly, she thought he meant he'd leave the matter to the police. He glanced at Kat, who pursed her lips in exasperation. Nothing got past her.

Well, guilt or not, he couldn't let this mystery go.

"We better get to the pottery stall." He wiggled out of his mother's embrace. Quickly, he patted his baby brother on the head, waved his mother goodbye and headed for the door.

CHAPTER 3
MARKET MADNESS

The usual crowds filled Thebes' narrow, dusty streets, growing thicker as they neared the city center.

Today, however, people seemed different. They seemed scared. Three women in gold-trimmed linen sheaths stood with their heads close together, whispering in frantic voices. A street-sweeper scanned this way and that with wide, frightened eyes, clutching his broom like a weapon.

The siblings neared a temple. Out front, several medjay police questioned a priest in urgent voices. Zet slowed, trying to eavesdrop. The air was thick with incense.

Kat yanked his elbow. "Come on! It's late. We have to get to the stall."

"Shh, let's listen," he whispered. "They're obviously talking about the mummy."

But the medjay had sharp ears. He turned and glared.

Zet had friends in the police force, having helped them solve several crimes. Unfortunately this officer, clad in a leopard-skin kilt with a club fastened at his waist, was a stranger.

"Move along," the medjay warned, hand on his club. "The pair of you."

"But we—"

"This is official business," the medjay said. "Keep walking."

"Come on," Kat said. "Let's go."

"We should tell him about last night. We should tell him that we saw the mummy. It might be helpful," Zet hissed. Plus, he wouldn't mind getting in a few questions of his own.

"No. We have customers waiting. You promised Mother. Besides, we can't afford to set tongues wagging again for opening late. This time, the market owner will kick us out for sure. And then we'll be in serious trouble. You know we can't afford to lose our stall."

She was right. He groaned out loud.

Then he took off at a run, sandals slapping the hot earth.

"Last one there is a rotten goose egg," he shouted.

He knew without glancing back that she was rolling her eyes. Still, she got there nearly as fast as he did.

"Only because you had a head start," she panted, hands on both knees.

Together they opened the stall's tent doors and lifted protective sheets from their wares. Inside, dishes of every size gleamed in the early light. There were bowls and cooking pots, vases and decorative pottery. The swish of curtains sent up puffs of dust as Zet tied them back.

From all around, other vendors' stalls clattered to life.

Spicy smells rose from a food takeaway nearby. Across the way, spices of every color were mounded in baskets. Fruits and vegetables shone brightly. Goats bleated and fishmongers laid out their catches. Shoppers filtered in, poking and prodding and haggling.

"Pots for sale!" Zet shouted, adding to the din. "Clay pots! Come and get your pots!"

But nothing could banish the mummy from his thoughts—the mummy and the strange chant and the way he'd pointed directly at their door. At *him*.

"Is it just me, or are people avoiding us?" Kat said.

It was true. To their dismay, not a single person came to buy their wares all morning. At midday, they sat in the shade behind stacks of pottery to eat lunch.

Zet shoveled chickpea salad into his mouth. Worried or not, nothing ever dampened his appetite. "People are definitely avoiding us."

"Why?" Kat said. "This is awful! Even with the Wag Festival coming, I'm not expecting a rush on fancy plates. It's not that sort of event. But we've never gone a single morning without selling a few cooking pots. They break all the time. Water jugs do, too. And clay bread loaf pans. What's going on?"

"I don't know. Could it have to do with the mummy?"

Kat's forehead wrinkled under her dark bangs. "Wait." Her face paled. *"Do you think the mummy actually cursed us?* Oh by the gods, I knew it was Aziza. I just knew it!"

"Nah," he muttered. He tried to push all thoughts of Pharaoh's cousin—bitter, vengeful Aziza—from his mind. "It's probably just a coincidence. We did *nothing* to him! That whole business wasn't our fault. Look, forget I said anything. Let's get back to work."

Lunch over, they returned to the front of the tent. As soon as they had, Kat grabbed Zet's arm and her fingers dug in hard.

"Ow!" Zet said.

"Look!" She pointed. "At that stack of plates."

Zet did as she said, seeing the pile of pottery that hadn't been there earlier.

"Someone's returned all of their dinnerware," she gasped.

Zet stared in shock. "Strange. They paid for them. Don't they want them anymore?"

As if in answer, a frantic-looking couple scuttled up with armloads of pottery. The man wore his wig low to cover his eyes. The woman hid her face behind a clay jug. She'd bought that jug only last week. Zet remembered selling it to her.

"You're bringing those back?" Zet asked, baffled. "Is something wrong?"

They made no reply. Instead, they set the pottery down and scurried off.

"Wait!" Zet called after them. "Let me give you some deben coins!"

The couple ignored his calls.

Zet sat heavily on an upside-down urn. He grabbed his head in both hands. "I have a bad feeling about this."

Kat said, "I was right! We are cursed! And everyone knows!"

"We're not cursed," Zet tried to insist.

At that moment, a woman inched up to the tent. She crouched down to abandon a beautiful serving dish. Before she got away, Kat caught the woman by her shawl.

"Please," Kat begged. "Don't leave."

"I must. Let go of me!"

"At least tell me why you're returning that dish," Kat begged.

The woman's face flushed scarlet. "My husband says it's unsafe to keep your platter in our house."

"Why?"

"Because of Aziza." She tried to disentangle her shawl from Kat's fingers.

Kat was nearly in tears. She held the woman fast. "But what does Aziza have to do with your platter?"

"Don't play coy. We both know Aziza never forgave you for that time your brother tripped him—in this very stall—and broke his nose on that jug."

"My brother didn't trip him, it was an accident! Why does no one believe that it was an accident?"

"Aziza was very particular about his looks. He used to be a handsome man, but after that? With everyone calling him Jugnose?"

"I never called him Jugnose," Kat said.

"Maybe not, but the rest of Thebes did. Is it any wonder he's come back from the dead to curse you?"

"I'm very sorry about his nose," Kat said earnestly. "But it was an accident!"

"As to that, I can't say," the woman sniffed.

"My lady," Zet said, "There's no reason to return your platter. Trust me, we're not cursed."

She scoffed. "Aziza was haunting your doorstep last night. With Anubis, snarling God of the Underworld, at his heels! And I have no intention of crossing either of them." The woman yanked her shawl free from Kat's hand.

"But—that doesn't make sense!" Zet protested, "Aziza can't return from the dead. That's not how it works!"

The woman hurried off.

"Wait," Zet called after her. "Let us at least refund your platter!" If they had to refund everyone's returns, they'd soon be poor. But what choice did he have? It was the right thing to do.

The woman ignored him and disappeared into the crowd.

Kat moaned. "Oh Zet, we're in huge trouble."

"This makes no sense," Zet said. "Aziza either made it to the Underworld, or the gods destroyed him at his judgment trial. He couldn't return to haunt us. No one can."

Kat looked at Zet. "I don't know."

He set his jaw. "I'm right and you know it. So let's hide away these returns. Because when this blows over, everyone's going to want their stuff back."

Kat blinked away tears. "We're cursed, Zet. Curses don't blow over."

Zet ignored wary stares from market-goers. "This is a mystery," he insisted. "And like any mystery, it can be solved." He picked up the abandoned platter. "Hey, don't worry. We'll figure it out. Now do you see why I need to investigate?"

Her tears turned to annoyance. She rubbed her face and finally blew out a sigh. "All right, yes. You win. We investigate. *Together.*"

CHAPTER 4
TROUBLE ON THE NILE

For two days, Zet and Kat scoured their street for clues. They tried to question the neighbors, but all ran away, shouting that they didn't want Aziza cursing them, too. At night the siblings slept in shifts, watching in vain for the mummy's return.

The mummy hadn't paid a second visit. The pottery returns kept piling up, though. And Apu kept crying and pointing out the front window like he was being haunted.

Today the market was closed. Zet and Kat were meeting up with their two best friends.

Hui, whom they'd known since birth, was a joker who loved getting into trouble. But he was also a highly skilled jewelers' apprentice who now worked in the royal foundry. Princess Meritamen, who they'd met on an earlier adventure, had become a fast friend. She loved sneaking out of the palace and pretending she was a normal kid. Still, caution forced her to wear a cloak that shadowed her face.

Maybe together they could come up with answers.

All four friends were gathered on a small river raft. Zet stood with both feet planted and shoved his bamboo pole into the Nile's rushing waters. Carefully, he guided them around a rock. Hui jabbed a fishing net into the water and came up empty. Ibis birds floated alongside, white feathers gleaming. Kat kicked her feet in the current as she chatted earnestly with Princess Meritamen, or Merit as she liked to be called.

Zet was working hard to keep the raft straight but found it hard to concentrate. He was too worried.

Hui lunged with the net. "Aw, missed again!" he cried.

"Uh huh," Zet agreed in a flat voice. "Hey, Merit, you don't believe we're cursed, do you?"

If anyone knew about curses, mummies, and burial secrets, Merit would. She was Pharaoh's daughter after all.

She scrunched her eyes in thought.

"We're in real trouble," Kat said. "If people keep returning their pottery, we'll be ruined."

"I'm so sorry. This is terrible," Merit said.

The raft flew downstream with the current.

Zet said, "Well, I don't believe the mummy was Aziza. There's no way he's come back from the dead. Not after facing the goddess, Maat at his judgment trial. You know what? I bet he used a scarab spell. So that his black heart weighed less than Maat's feather of truth. It's the only way grumpy old Jugnose could make it into the Great Beyond."

"Zet!" Kat hissed, "Don't call him that."

Hui said, "Maybe he didn't make it to the Great Beyond." In a spooky voice, he added, "Maybe Maat's tossed his rotten heart to Ammit. *Devourer of the Dead.* They say it has the legs of a hippo, the front paws of a lion, and the head of a crocodile. And when you fail the judgment test, it snatches your heart, chews it up and swallows it. *Poof*, it's all over. No afterlife for you. I bet *that's* what happened to Aziza."

Kat made a face. "Gruesome."

Hui waggled his brows at her. "Really? Are you scared?"

She crossed her arms. "Of course I'm not scared. I don't have a wicked heart. Not like some people I know."

Hui looked wildly offended. "What's that supposed to mean?"

Zet rolled his eyes. Merit snickered. But Hui had a point.

"Either way, whether he passed the test or if Ammit finished him off," Zet said, "He couldn't be haunting us."

"True." Hui rubbed his shaved scalp.

"Right, Merit?" Zet said.

For the second time that morning, she simply squinted away at some sunny spot downriver. Water lapped at the raft's edges. Zet pushed off the bottom again with the paddle. He stayed close to shore, keeping an eye out for dangers like crocodiles and hippos.

"Right, Merit?" Zet prompted.

She pulled her knees up and turned to face them. "I shouldn't tell you this because it's secret knowledge."

Hui sat forward, his eyes wide. "Really? Now you have to!"

She trailed her feet in the water in silence. Finally, she said, "I'm only speaking of this because I feel you have a right to know. Priests have created certain spells that can be written on tomb walls. They . . ."

Hui sat further forward. "They what?"

"They awaken the mummy. So that he can haunt and kill his enemies."

Kat let out a small cry.

Shaken, Zet shouted, "We weren't Aziza's enemies."

"Awaken the mummy," Hui cried, dropping his net and scanning the riverbank. "What does the spell say? Tell me exactly what it says."

Merit recited it in a low, clear voice, ending with the final, awful verse: "*I shall seize his neck like that of a goose. I shall make him miserable. I shall make him die from hunger and thirst.*"

A spooked silence fell.

Kat had turned pale.

Zet spoke up. "But we didn't do anything to him! It was an accident."

Making a face, Hui said. "Aziza didn't see it that way."

Merit spoke up. "There's another problem."

"Another problem?" Kat asked in a high, worried voice.

"You said a jackal was guarding the mummy. So Anubis, God of the Underworld, has taken his earthly form. That doesn't bode well, I'm afraid."

Zet tried to swallow the lump in his throat. "Oh?"

"If this mummy has returned to the living, it has done so with the blessing of Anubis. If the God of the Underworld has appeared in the form of a jackal . . ."

Hui got unsteadily to his bare feet as if he could sit still no longer. The raft had drifted into a fast-moving current. It rocked under him as they sped along. "So what are you saying?"

"The God of Death walks amongst us," Merit whispered. "People are right to be afraid. Egypt is in danger. We cannot forget that we're at war in the north. The army is the only thing holding back the Hyksos invaders. We need the gods on our side."

Zet thought of his father, a soldier on the front lines. His chest tightened. Hui's father was up there fighting, too.

Merit's ringed fingers tugged at one another in turn.

Their raft had sailed far from the noisy watersteps, where fishermen unloaded their catches. Here in a lonely river bend, reeds grew tall along the shore. The dashing current gurgled and slapped the plants.

A mud-brick wall came into view. It barricaded the right bank. Beyond the wall, city buildings loomed in the sun's glare. The nearest one, the Royal Treasury, rose higher than the rest.

Merit nodded at the Treasury. "Wars are expensive. I'm afraid I overheard my father say funds are running low. Without funds, we can't get supplies to our troops."

Everyone followed her gaze.

"If Anubis has come to Thebes," Merit said. "If he's angry, the God of Death could plunge us into terrible trouble. Our soldiers are the only thing holding off the invaders."

Zet struggled to find his voice. "Merit, you need to stay away from us. We need to turn around! If you get cursed because of us—if—"

"Stay away?" Her eyes flashed. "I am a royal daughter. I would never stand down when Egypt's people are in trouble. Let alone abandon my best friends."

Zet started to argue.

The raft slammed into some unmoving object.

The force threw Hui flat on his face next to Kat. Hui's hands shot out and Kat grabbed them. They held on to keep from falling over the edge.

The jarring halt sent Zet flying. He shouted in horror as Princess Meritamen tumbled off the raft.

With an awful splash, Merit hit the water. A hundred things flashed through Zet's mind. Most of all, he was thinking of the hippopotamus, the river's deadliest animal. If its massive jaws didn't crush you, it would drown you underfoot.

Merit's eyes met his for one brief, awful moment.

Then, she was sucked beneath the brown, swirling surface.

CHAPTER 5
A STRANGE PAIR

"Merit!" Zet shouted.

He jumped in, his feet striking the murky bottom. The Nile waters rose to his chest. He plunged under, searching desperately for the Princess in the silty brown current.

Nothing.

"Merit!" Kat shrieked.

Suddenly there came a splash as Merit popped up a dozen paces away. She coughed and sputtered and stood unsteadily in the rushing current.

Zet plunged toward her. Crocodiles lurked in shallow places like this. They'd lie in wait, with only their eyes and snouts jutting into the air. And they pounced fast.

"Quick, back on the raft!" Zet shouted, pushing her forward.

"Give us your hands," Kat cried.

She and Hui hauled Zet and Merit back aboard. The four stood dripping and breathing hard.

Zet said, "We better get moving, we're like sitting ducks."

He pushed off with the pole. The raft wouldn't budge.

"What's happening?" Kat demanded.

Hui reached a cautious hand into the water. "We're stuck on a rock."

Merit said, "This is odd. I boated here last week in the royal barge and the Nile was deep. It shouldn't be shallow. Look at that sandbank, where did all that sand come from?"

"I don't know." Zet glanced around, feeling uneasy. It was a great responsibility to have Merit out here. "Let's free the raft and get back. I don't like this."

None of them did. They exchanged spooked glances.

Warily, the four children slid into the river. They shoved hard, but the raft was waterlogged and heavy. The lashings were stuck firm.

Movement on the riverbank made Zet turn and look.

On shore stood a rough-skinned woman with long hair and narrowed eyes. Tall grasses swayed up to her strong shoulders. She leaned out, holding a fishing net, and threw it onto the water.

"Hey!" Zet called. "Hello—my lady!"

The woman gave him the evil eye and waved the children away.

"We're stuck," Zet called, ignoring her glares. "Can you help us push off?"

That's when he noticed a small hut, partially hidden in the lush overgrowth. The door flew open and a huge man thrust his way outside. His muscular arms held a heavy-looking bucket. An enormous blade gleamed at his waist. It looked sharp and deadly.

"Here now," growled the man. "What's all this shouting?"

"It's those noisy children." The woman made a sour face. "Get rid of them."

"What's the trouble?" the man thundered.

Zet, Kat, Hui, and Merit exchanged worried glances. Water surged around their legs.

"We're stuck on a rock," Zet called back. "We need some help."

The man set down his basket. He wiped his hands on his barrel chest and waded into the Nile. "This is men's work. Outta my way, girls," he sneered. But then his eyes fastened on Merit and he studied her face as if trying to place the Princess.

Kat quickly whispered, "Pull your hood over your head."

Zet had to get Merit away from him. "I better walk the girls to shore. We're crocodile bait out here. I'll be back."

The man grunted but watched them go. Had he recognized Merit? Even though he'd agreed to help, this couple seemed strange. Merit had already been kidnapped once before.

As the three children sloshed on shore, Zet was dismayed when Kat and Merit restarted their earlier conversation about the mummy, for the woman's ears perked up.

"What's all this about a mummy?" she asked sharply.

"Oh . . ." Kat said, stopping short. "You . . . haven't heard?"

Zet elbowed her.

"Tell me," the woman cooed.

Kat bit her lip, glancing at Zet.

"Come now, don't leave me in the dark," the woman complained. "A mummy is cursing people? You'd better tell me. I'm a citizen, too. And my good husband is helping you, after all."

Reluctantly, Kat described the haunting. The woman clucked her tongue. As Kat spoke, Zet's eyes fell on what looked like an old stone building block that looked like part of a foundation. Odd.

Was that hieroglyphic writing carved on its surface?

Why would a fancy rock be lying here by the river?

Zet edged closer for a better look. The woman, however, pushed in front of him and sat heavily on the stone block. She spread her dirty linen skirt around her, covering the hieroglyphics. Was she hiding them? Or did it just seem that way?

He opened his mouth to ask about the stone when a great roar from the river made him spin around. The huge man had lifted the raft halfway out of the water.

"There!" the man shouted. "Now get lost, you kids. Stop bothering us poor fisher-folk."

Hui waved frantically. "Let's go!"

Zet and the girls were happy to comply. Before leaving the shore, Zet uprooted two sturdy reeds and lugged them onto the raft.

"Lucky you didn't get eaten by a crocodile, lots of 'em down here," the man told Merit in a sneering tone.

"Yes, very lucky, thank you," she said.

He helped her roughly onto the raft, giving her a small shove. "The river's a bad place for a bunch of pampered kids. Stay away if you know what's good for you."

Zet feared setting the man off, so he tried for an even tone. "Thanks for your help."

"Yes," the others chimed in. "Thank you."

Using the extra reeds as poles, the children worked together to make their way back upstream.

Zet said, "Last time you boated here, Merit, did you see that couple?"

"No." She shook her head. "But fishermen come and go. I still wonder what made that sandbank in the middle of the river, though."

They finally reached the shore from where they'd first set out. Together, the children beached the raft. Using an old rope, they tied it to a gnarled acacia tree.

"Mother will be worried," Kat said, glancing at the darkening sky. "It's late. Getting unstuck took a long time."

"I'll accompany Merit back to the palace," Zet said. "You two go home and tell everyone we're fine."

Hui nodded. "All right."

The four made none of their usual noisy goodbyes. Too many worries hung over them. Zet and Merit watched Kat and Hui melt into the shadows, then headed for the palace.

As they hurried through the nightfall, stars winked to life. Zet couldn't help worrying about his father and the warning the Princess had issued earlier that day.

He turned to her. "So treasury funds are really running low?"

"I'm afraid so," Merit said.

"Will you have enough to support the army? My father is up there. Hui's is, too."

"I know. Fortunately, when we gather the taxes from the coming harvest, they should replenish some of our funds. But if something happens to destroy the harvest . . ."

"You mean, like an angry Anubis?" Zet said.

"Exactly."

"The medjay police are out questioning priests about the jackal and the mummy. They must be worried, too."

Merit nodded. "The medjay police are on alert. But getting to the bottom of this problem is the Royal Guard's duty. The mummy falls under religious disturbances—which fall under the realm of Pharaoh the Living God."

"The Royal Guard! But if they're busy investigating the mummy, who's protecting the Treasury? Isn't that their job?"

"It would be near impossible to break into that building. Only a few Royal Guards are needed to protect the Treasury."

Zet breathed a sigh of relief. At least the Treasury was safe. He didn't need to worry about things he couldn't control. He needed to focus on two things: putting an end to the problems at the pottery stall and stopping that mummy from haunting Thebes.

They reached the palace wall. Here, they'd have to say goodbye, for he wasn't supposed to enter the Royal Grounds without Pharaoh's permission. He'd help Merit over the wall, but she'd have to run across the lawns and sneak back into the palace on her own.

Merit brushed her dark hair from her eyes. Jewels glowed on her ringed fingers in the moonlight. "I want you to climb over with me."

He hid his surprise, but then understood. "Of course. Your people must know you're missing by now. It's my fault. We never should have convinced you to come out on the raft. I'll talk to your father." Even if the threat of Pharaoh's anger made his short hair stand on end.

She grinned. "Thanks, but no—I'll have to face my father myself. And it's certainly not your fault. There *is* someone else I'd like you to talk to, though."

"Who?"

"You'll see. Will it be all right if you stay out a little longer?"

He laughed. "If you're going to be in trouble, I might as well be, too."

CHAPTER 6
MUMMIFICATION SECRETS

Together, Zet and Merit clambered over the wall and dropped onto the palace grounds. They were in a quiet grove of citrus trees. In the distance, lamps twinkled in the palace.

"Who goes there?" came a sentry's voice.

"Stand down," Merit called. "It's me. Princess Meritamen."

The sentry approached. Bowing low, he said, "Your Highness."

She smiled. "There's no trouble here. Have a good evening."

The sentry moved out of earshot.

"Seems I haven't been missed." She sighed with obvious relief. "I suppose my ruse worked. Which means we still have time."

He didn't ask about her ruse. "Time for what?"

"Answers." Instead of heading for the palace, she guided him around a small lake. A temple stood in the distance. "Hurry."

Merit broke into a run. Zet fell into step beside her willowy form. Soon, the temple loomed over them. Rather than entering, Merit skirted past the temple. She kept going until they reached a small stone building around back. The cane door was shut. Lamplight spilled through narrow cracks. Merit made to knock and then paused.

Inside, a man chanted. Gooseflesh rose on Zet's arms. *A prayer? Or a spell?*

Merit pressed her eye to a crack. Zet did the same. He nearly gasped out loud. Clapping a hand over his mouth, he stared at the shadowy form inside.

The figure towered almost to the ceiling. He had a man's body, but his head . . . by the gods! He had the head of a *jackal!*

Pointy ears. A long snout. Canine teeth. Sleek fur over a muscled jaw.

"Anubis!" Zet hissed, unable to help himself.

The divine figure stiffened. He turned and stared at the door. "Who DARES disturb me?" boomed the God of Death. Anubis took three giant strides and threw the door open.

Zet cringed and fell at Anubis's feet. He covered his face with both hands.

By the wings of Isis, this was it. They were dead. It was all over!

The deep voice boomed, "Princess Meritamen?"

Face still pressed to the dirt, Zet's brow wrinkled. Anubis knew Merit's name?

"High Priest," she said. "I'm sorry to disturb your work."

High Priest?

Zet risked a glance upward. The figure untied a chinstrap and removed the jackal's head. This was no god. He was a man in a mask. Thank Ra!

"You should not see me like this." Angered, the High Priest set the mask aside. "Even if you are the Daughter of a Living God. And that boy should be punished!"

"I brought him," Merit said. "I'm responsible. He's under my protection."

The priest pinned Zet with a cold stare. To Merit, he said, "Why have you come?"

"It's an emergency."

"Indeed?" The priest frowned.

Zet, unable to hold his tongue, blurted, "Why were you dressed like Anubis?"

The priest shot Zet a sour look. "You've seen me. I suppose there's no point in keeping it secret. I am the Royal Mummifier.

When I make a mummy, I wear the mask of Anubis. That way, the Jackal-Headed God's magic works through me to preserve the dead for the Afterlife."

"But no one has died." Merit's hand went to her mouth. "Have they?"

"Rest easy, Princess. It was a sacred temple cat. I'm sending her on to Bastet, the Cat Goddess who watches over home and hearth. Now, what's this emergency?"

"We need to learn about mummies," she said.

He drew himself up and towered over them. "That's priest's knowledge!"

Now it was her turn to straighten to her full height. Her eyes flashed. "I am Princess Meritamen. Royal Daughter. Child of the Lord of the Two Lands, Descendant of the High Priest of Every Temple, Daughter of the Living God himself! Will you defy me?"

Zet's eyes widened. He'd never seen her this way. For the first time, he truly realized that she was more than just his friend.

Lamplight flickered behind the Mummifier.

Finally, the priest said, "This boy is not royal. I cannot speak in front of him."

Zet smiled awkwardly.

Merit said, "His name is Zet. He's the famous boy who came to my rescue once before. He's saved Pharaoh, too. He's solved many crimes. And I've asked him to help solve the mummy mystery that's haunting all of Thebes."

Zet couldn't help thinking it sounded pretty good when she said it like that. He practically glowed.

"Doesn't look like much of a hero to me," the priest said.

Zet's glow turned to embarrassment.

Merit said, "He has my royal blessing. So will you help us? I'm sure you don't want me to trouble my father. But I could wake my Royal Grandmother and bring her down here."

Now it was the priest's turn to look awkward. Zet stifled a laugh.

"Oh, very well," the priest said. "But come inside and shut the door. The sacred Wag Festival of the Dead approaches. With it, the veil between life and death grows thin. Restless spirits draw near when a mummy is being made. Even the mummy of a small cat."

As they squeezed inside the hut, Zet's mind went to last year's Wag Festival. Like always, the people of Thebes had lined up along the Nile. They'd brought tiny paper boats, hundreds and hundreds of them. Each boat was a tribute to Osiris, the Mummified God who was Egypt's first mummy. People also made tributes to those who'd passed into the Afterlife. The boats had floated in a bright flotilla. Kat had called them pretty. Now, however, with a mummy on the loose, the coming Wag Festival of the Dead unsettled him.

Zet quickly closed the door.

Inside, smoke drifted from the lamp. It cast a haze over the assembled tools, worktables, and containers. Zet shuddered. Merit did the same.

"Now." The priest tapped his gnarled index finger on his worktable. "How will sharing my secret arts help you solve this mystery?"

Merit said, "Zet? Please go ahead and ask what you need."

"I'm grateful for anything you can tell me," Zet said.

The priest's deep-set eyes were like two black hollows. "I will tell you," he said. "But you must promise to never repeat what you hear tonight."

"I promise," Zet and Merit said at once.

Shadows played in the creases of the priest's lined face. "Then I will begin."

Zet and Merit stood spellbound as the priest lifted a mummified object from the table. It was tubular, around a foot long, and wrapped neatly from end to end. On closer inspection, it was almost doll-like. The priest had given the tiny mummy pointy cat ears made from linen strips. He'd drawn a cat's face, too.

Instead of being scary, the mummy was almost cute.

Zet's thoughts went to their family shrine honoring Bastet. He loved their Cat Goddess statue. He often rubbed its glossy black head and spoke to it when worried. Now, he couldn't help making a silent prayer to Bastet to keep this temple cat safe until she reached the playful fields of the Afterlife.

Perhaps the High Priest noticed, for he paused a moment before clearing his throat. "This mummy, like all mummies, took seventy days to create. There are many steps. I will explain."

Zet and Merit nodded in earnest.

"First, the body is carefully washed and purified. Second . . . " He paused, eyeing Zet and Merit as if daring them not to faint. "We cut out the organs. The lungs, the intestines, the stomach, the liver. Of course, we're not butchers. We do try to keep the body looking whole."

"That sounds hard," Zet said, ignoring his churning stomach.

"It is." From a tray, the priest lifted a hooked stick. "We push this long instrument up the nose and stir it around." He demonstrated in the air, gyrating the stick with great force. "Do you know why?"

Wincing, Zet and Merit shook their heads.

"To mash up the brain and pick it out of the nostrils."

"*Eeeew,*" Merit said.

Zet leaned in. "What do you do with the brain?"

The High Priest leaned forward, too. "We throw it away."

"Throw it away?" Zet asked. "Where?"

"The garbage. The brain has no purpose."

Merit crossed her arms. "And then what do you do?"

He seemed almost disappointed at being unable to spook them. "The stomach, lungs, liver, and intestines are stored in what we call canopic jars. Each jar is guarded by a god whose head is carved on the lid. Next, when the body's empty, we stuff it with linen. That's to keep it plumped up. We then soak it in natron salts for forty days."

"Why?" Merit asked.

"We want to dry it out, to prevent rot. Now, when the body is dry, we wrap the mummy in yards of bandages—it's a long process. Partly because we tuck magic-spell amulets into the linen strips." He made tucking motion.

"Magic amulets?" Zet said, sharing a glance with Merit.

"Indeed. Each one must be activated by chanting a prayer. Then the mummy is placed in a sarcophagus and we fasten a carved death mask over the mummy's face." He seemed enraptured by his own words, as though this was the first time he'd ever had anyone to tell them to.

Zet said, "Did you perform the honorable Aziza's mummification?"

The priest looked startled. A shadow fell over his hawk-like eyes. "Why do you ask?"

"You must've heard what people are saying—that the haunted mummy is Pharaoh's cousin returned from the dead."

"I don't listen to gossip." He fussed with his tools.

Merit spoke up. "You said magic amulets are tucked into a mummy's wrappings. Could Aziza's amulets help him curse his enemies?"

The priest stroked the cat mummy's ears in silence.

"Could he have come back from the dead?" Merit prodded. "Like everyone's saying?"

In a clipped voice, the priest said, "I did not preside over Aziza's mummification. I was not told what spells were used."

"But is it possible?" Merit said.

"Do you dare question the powers of Anubis? Of course it's possible. But would it be done? That, I cannot tell you, Princess."

Zet said, "Why not? Why won't you say?"

"I humbly ask that you leave so I may get back to my work." Instead of humble, however, his words sounded almost threatening.

Was the priest hiding something? Did he honestly know nothing of Aziza's royal burial? Even though it had happened only recently?

The priest donned his frightening Anubis mask. The huge jackal's head with its gleaming teeth caused Merit and Zet to back away. Zet had nearly forgotten that this man was a servant of Anubis, God of Death. That was a frightening thought.

"My thanks, priest," Merit said. "We will leave you. My blessings are upon you." She took Zet's arm and they hurried back outside.

A chill gripped the night. Or maybe the sinister priest's presence had turned Zet cold.

Merit kept going until they reached the lake's far side as if trying to distance themselves from the servant of Anubis.

Yet the black, starlit water seemed poor protection from the ominous mysteries swirling around them.

CHAPTER 7
NO MORE SECRETS

Merit sat down by the water, breathing hard. "I hope my father doesn't hear about this!"

"But you said—"

"If he found out I was grilling the High Priest of Mummification for sacred secrets, he'd double my attendants. And I wouldn't be climbing over any more walls!" She rubbed her shins. "He's told me to act more regal. Awful, isn't it? You heard that there's a statue of me going up outside the Temple of Isis next week?"

"Yes."

She grimaced. "Everyone in Thebes will recognize my face after that. I won't be able to go anywhere."

Zet sank down next to her. "I wish I could do something to help."

"You can't. That's just how life is."

Zet glanced at the temple from where they'd come. In the light of the half-moon, the lake waters looked black.

"Do you think that priest was hiding something? About Aziza?" he asked.

"I'm not sure. I doubt it."

Zet scratched his neck. The priest had been so abrupt when he'd asked whether Aziza's mummy could come back to life. He shivered, recalling the mummy on his doorstep, the way it pointed at him with its bony finger, and that awful whispered incantation. And how Apu hadn't stopped crying since.

By the gods, he should have asked how to get rid of a mummy's curse!

He turned to tell Merit that he needed to go back and demand more answers. But Merit spoke first.

"I need to get back," she said. Worry seemed to lie heavily on her regal shoulders. And responsibility.

He was again reminded that Merit was more than a friend. She was a royal daughter.

He nodded. "Good night, Princess."

"Good night, Zet. Go safely."

Zet ran toward home.

All throughout Thebes, doors and windows were shut tight. Fear hung in the air.

Unlike most people, however, Zet longed for a glimpse of the mummy. He wanted to chase the monster down. He wanted answers.

Zet reached his street, panting, and sped up the steps to his house. At the door, he paused. *Mother was going to be furious!*

From outside, Apu could be heard crying. Zet took a big breath and pushed open the door. His mother rushed from the kitchen. Kat, who held the wailing Apu, followed.

"Where were you?" his mother cried. "Kat said you went to the palace hours ago! What happened? Did you see the mummy again?"

"No," he said. "Merit asked me to help her with something and—" He broke off. Now was probably as good a time as any to tell her about the stall. "Mother, I have bad news."

"If you're talking about the pottery returns, I know all about it."

Zet glanced at Kat. "You told her?"

Kat looked equally surprised. "Not me!"

"Children, did you really think you could keep it from me? What were you thinking, hiding such a thing?"

"We—" Zet said, but she cut him off.

"I know that after I had Apu, I was unwell. With your father away, I had no choice but to let you manage the stall."

"And you said we were doing a good job!" Kat said.

"Yes, but now I see it's foolish to let you continue."

"But mother!" Zet said. "We're good at it."

"You are hiding things from me. I had to find out about the pottery from a neighbor. Do you have any idea how embarrassing that was?"

"We would have told you," Zet said, "But we didn't want you to be worried!"

"Enough." She turned and swept Apu from Kat's arms. "Tomorrow, we'll all go to the market. We'll bring the pottery returns home and close up shop until this . . . this cursed mummy . . . is sorted out by the medjay police."

Zet said, "Princess Meritamen asked me to help solve the mystery."

His mother's sharp intake of breath seemed to suck the air from the room. In the silence that followed, only Apu's soft sniffles could be heard.

Finally, his mother said, "I wish she hadn't done that."

"But she's the Princess, mother! I can't say no." And he didn't want to. "Besides, all of Thebes is saying we're cursed." He glanced at the sniffling Apu, worried but not wanting to say anything. Apu, red-cheeked, seemed to gasp for breath before making another sob. "We have to do something."

His mother walked away and could be heard setting Apu on his kitchen play mat.

Zet and Kat shared a glance.

Their mother returned wearing a resigned expression. With a sigh, she put a gentle hand on Zet's shoulder. "You are my oldest son. And like your fearless father, I worry you're too brave for your own good."

"How about me?" Kat asked. "What am I?"

Their mother's brows went up and she shook her head. "Oh children, what am I to do with you?"

"If I'm not brave, what am I?" Kat wanted to know.

Zet rolled his eyes.

"Kat, you are my beautiful daughter. And sometimes I fear you're too smart for your own good. And I love you both very much. That's why I worry."

The scent of dinner wafted from the kitchen in the back. Zet's stomach growled. He realized he hadn't eaten in hours. He was starving.

"Now come, let's eat," she said.

In the kitchen's cozy glow, the family pulled up cushions. They sat in a small circle. The simple act made Zet feel safe. Kat's shoulders relaxed. Their mother steered their chatter to comforting topics. Zet wolfed down warm, savory stew and thick slices of freshly baked bread, refusing to think about the threat of hungrier days ahead. Even Apu seemed slightly mollified as he chewed on a piece of cucumber.

After dinner, their mother laid out a game of senet. They took turns rolling the bones, trying to best each other and even laughing. For a time, their fears were banished to the shadows outside.

But when their mother kissed them good night, the fearsome shadows came creeping back. As Zet climbed the ladder to the roof, he noticed a mummy-shaped outline in one corner, causing him to look twice. It was just the old vase.

Kat paused on the bottom step. "Mother, what if we really are cursed? I'm scared."

"Come here." She hugged Kat. "Who could ever curse you, my perfect daughter?"

Until tonight, Zet would have agreed. The idea had seemed crazy. But meeting the Mummifier had shaken him.

Aziza could, Zet thought. *Aziza could have cursed us all.*

CHAPTER 8
A GROUP EFFORT

The following day dawned bright and hot. The sun god, Ra, shone over the market. The mountains of returned pottery gleamed in the light.

Sounds of chaos soon filled the stall. For the first time in days, however, this chaos was of their own making.

Zet, Kat, their mother, and Apu were there. Hui, unfortunately, was busy at the royal foundry but his mother Delilah, had come to help. And she'd brought Hui's four rowdy little brothers.

The small boys raced around, shouting. Some tried to stand on their heads. Others dangled from tent poles. Hui's mother, meanwhile, was a whirlwind herself: she yelled at her children, packed pottery, and scolded customers who dared approach with more returns.

All day long, the two families carted pottery back to Zet and Kat's house and stored it in the front room. By mid-afternoon, their house was overflowing, and Zet and Kat were exhausted. Still, they headed to the market for another run.

"Hey, you know what?" Zet said as they passed what he realized was Aziza's street. "We should detour past Aziza's old house."

Kat paled. "Don't you think it's been sold?"

"Maybe not. We should have thought of this before. We might find some clues."

Kat frowned. "What kind of clues?"

Zet said, "I'm not sure. Let's sneak in and look around."

"Break in? Are you crazy?" Kat swiped the bangs from her eyes. "What if Mother finds out? She's just forgiven us. No, don't be stupid."

"Stupid? Well, sorr-ee, Miss Perfect, but do you want to solve this or not?"

Kat glared. "Of course I want to solve this. But what if it's haunted? I bet you didn't think of that."

"That would be bad," Zet admitted. "Oh, come on, we're out of options."

"I don't know."

"Unless you have a better idea?"

"Fine. A quick look," she said. "Let's hurry before we're missed."

They started running.

Suddenly, Kat slowed and her voice went up an octave. "What if we find Aziza's mummy asleep in his house? What if he's staying there and only comes out at night?"

Zet halted, picturing Aziza's mummy in a death-sleep with a massive jackal stretched out at his feet. Forcefully, he said. "I doubt he's in there."

Or so he hoped.

"I just had an idea." Kat's eyes had gone all big. "How about this? Every home has a household god, right? Like we have Bastet."

Zet nodded, thinking of their ebony Cat Goddess statue back home. "And?"

Despite her pale face, Kat looked determined. "If we can get into Aziza's house, we can learn the name of his household god. We could make offerings, so the god takes pity on us and stops Aziza from haunting us!"

"Huh. You know . . . At this point, anything is worth a try."

Together, they ran across the hot paving stones. A cluster of pigeons rose flapping into the air. They crossed through a dusty inter-section and skidded to a stop.

Men in uniform jammed the lane. More swarmed around Aziza's sprawling house. Most wore the colors of the Royal Guard.

Kat gasped. "Does this mean what I think it does?"

Zet's throat went dry. "The Royal Guards think Aziza really is the mummy."

"So Aziza *has* come back to curse our family. All because of that stupid jugnose business. I knew it!"

Zet fixed his attention on a big man dressed in a medjay police uniform. "Look." He grabbed his sister's arm and pointed at the offi-cer. "It's Merimose! Maybe he'll tell us what's going on."

Zet and Kat had helped Merimose solve a few mysteries. Still, the medjay wasn't always happy about it. He liked to complain about them getting underfoot.

Zet and Kat hurried toward him.

Merimose swung around. "Keep away!" he shouted, making a chopping motion.

"Merimose!" they called.

Recognizing them, he crossed his muscular arms over his broad chest. "Zet. Kat," he growled. "I wondered when you'd show up."

"Hi, Merimose," they said.

"I'm on duty. I can't talk," Merimose said.

Despite this, Zet reached to shake hands and the man accepted. The medjay's palm was the size of a dinner platter and the texture of old leather.

Kat said, "What's happening? Is Aziza in there?"

Merimose regarded her. "It's not my investigation. Not this time. The Royal Guards are in charge, not us medjay police."

Zet said, "Why are they searching Aziza's house?"

"You two need to stay out of this," Merimose boomed in his low voice.

"We can't!" Kat said. "Everyone knows Aziza is haunting us!"

A man's sharp voice rang out behind Zet. "Merimose! Get rid of those kids. Do your job!"

Zet whipped around and came face-to-face with a massive Royal Guard. The man wore a gold-embossed breastplate. A long, curved knife gleamed at his waist and he carried a lightweight, fiber shield.

Zet bowed quickly. "Sir, we're the family that Aziza is haunting."

Kat said, "Please, tell us what's going on!"

The man's brows came together to form what looked like a giant black caterpillar. "Leave. Now."

"But sir, we can help—" Zet began.

"NOW!" the Royal Guard barked.

"Renni." Merimose hooked one thumb in the leather waistband of his kilt. "If you don't mind, I'll handle this. I'm familiar with these two. They mean no harm."

"Harrumph!" the Royal Guard said.

Zet swallowed. He had to try one last time. "We've solved mysteries before. And Aziza is haunting us. Surely we can help! It was our jug that—"

"HOW DARE YOU?" the man roared. "I am the head of the Royal Guard. Pharaoh himself appointed me protector of Egypt. I am an instrument of the Gods. If I wish to speak to you, it will be at the time of my choosing."

Zet wanted to explain that the Princess had asked for his help. But he knew better. What if he got Merit into trouble? He wanted to at least tell Renni about the mummy's visit to their street. But the man strode away. He slammed through Aziza's front door and was gone.

Kat said, "I can't believe he wouldn't listen to what we had to say!"

Merimose, however, looked unsurprised.

The scent of baking bread drifted from a neighbor's house. The medjay's stomach made a loud gurgle. He rubbed his belly. "Sorry, didn't have time for lunch."

Kat pulled a small packet from her pocket. "I have some dried figs here."

Merimose accepted a handful and wolfed them down. Swallowing, he said, "Thanks. Now you'd better move along and let me do my job."

Kat tugged at her braids, looking uncertain and worried. "We're in big trouble, Merimose."

"People are shunning our pottery stall," Zet added. "Pretty soon, we'll be out of business. Our family won't be able to put food on the table. Or keep a roof over our heads. We need this sorted out. Fast."

"Let the Royal Guard do that. Be patient."

"Patient?" Kat cried. "You wouldn't say that if you'd seen our mountain of returned pottery. And you especially wouldn't say it if a scary monster was after you."

Merimose grew stern. "Here now! Don't you go trying to track down that mummy."

"Why not?" Zet said.

A muscle flexed in Merimose's jaw. "I don't know what's behind this. But if a mummy is walking the streets . . . and if that mummy was once Aziza . . . well, it's no longer Aziza—not anymore. I don't want you kids anywhere near it. Hear me?"

Zet swallowed.

Merimose said, "This is no joke. It's not some mystery for you to solve. A mummy is more than dangerous. It's a creature of death."

Kat seemed to shrink into herself.

"But—" Zet began.

"No, Zet. What can you do to stop it? A mummy can curse you with a whisper. It can kill you with a touch. You want to chase it down? Then what? Put your hands on its body, and you'll turn to dust."

The way he spoke sent a cold trickle down Zet's neck.

Merimose went on. "The Royal Guards are protected by the priests. But you and me? Our weapons mean nothing. Renni and his men are the only ones who can solve this. That's why I've ordered my men to stand down." He grasped them both by the shoulders. "Stay away. That's not a suggestion. It's an order. Stay far away."

"Don't worry," Kat said in a pinched voice. "We will."

Zet's mind raced back to the mummy's awful whispers. Already, it seemed to have cursed their stall. Was Apu already cursed?

Zet was only a boy. He wasn't a holy man. He desperately wanted to fight, but what could he do? It could make things worse. Much worse.

He glanced at Aziza's dark, cavernous house.

Merimose had ordered his men to stand down. So who was Zet to think he could end this haunting?

He stared at the ground. "I see what you mean. I only hope the Royal Guard can fix this. Before something worse happens."

CHAPTER 9

THE MUMMY STRIKES AGAIN

The Moon God, Khonsu, rose slowly in the evening sky.

Zet was pacing the rooftop when distant shouts drifted up from the streets below. He cocked his head, listening as the rising tide of babble swept closer.

Alarmed, he clambered downstairs, threw open their front door and ran outside. His mother and Kat followed close behind.

In the street, their neighbors stood in groups, talking in frightened voices.

Paneb, the brickmaker who lived next door, yelled, "Everyone get inside, lock your doors."

This only drew out more neighbors, all of them speaking at once.

Zet dashed up to the brickmaker. "What's going on?"

"Paneb?" his mother cried, "What's happened?"

Paneb was an honest man and a hard worker. Unlike other neighbors, he hadn't shunned Zet's family. In his raspy voice, he said, "The mummy is walking the streets again."

Zet looked around. "Here?"

"No—just off the Southern Road."

"The Southern Road?" A sick feeling struck the pit of Zet's stomach. "Uh oh."

SCOTT PETERS

Paneb said, "In Kanup Street."

"*Kanup Street?*" Kat screeched. "But that's where our friend Hui lives!"

Zet's hands went to his head. He didn't want to even think about what this meant. "I better go. It's attacking our friends. Mother, I'm going there."

"No," she said in a sharp voice. "You won't. I will alert the medjay."

"You can't leave. What about Apu? What if the mummy comes here?" Zet said.

Kat knotted the front of her nightdress. "The mummy must have gone to Hui's house because his mother helped us cart all that pottery back here."

"What do you mean?" their mother asked.

But Kat's words echoed Zet's own fears.

"Don't you see?" Kat's chin trembled. "The mummy is cursing Hui's family for helping us at the stall. Aziza is angry at them, now, too."

Paneb began backing toward his house. "You have no proof of that."

"By the gods!" Zet kicked his bare foot at the ground. "What if Kat's right? Mother, someone has to go. It has to be me."

"Fine." She nodded. A quick, jerky movement. "You will go for the medjay. Understood? Then come back to me safely. Now quick. Go."

Zet sprinted between the small crowd that had gathered. They parted to let him through. He rounded the corner and silence closed around him. Out of the darkness, he thought he heard footsteps. He drew to a halt. Yes, there they were. Coming up behind him.

He spun but there was no mummy, only the narrow silhouette of Kat in the moonlight. She was running hard.

"Kat!" he groaned. "You have to stay with Mother and Apu."

Her reply was heated. "Don't tell me what to do. Hui's my friend, too."

"Fine. But I'm not running for the medjay. Who knows how long they'd take. I'm going to Hui's. So let's just get there."

They reached the Southern Road. They were both panting by the time they turned into Kanup Street. Lamps blazed in every window and door. The crowds were thicker than at any festival in the Grand Plaza. Clearly, the mummy was long gone, but what had it done to Hui and his family? Had it hurt them?

"The back way, come on," Zet said.

They cut across a side street. Together, they clambered over the wall into Hui's tiny garden. Delilah was expecting them. She stood in the backyard with one hand on her hip.

"Not a step further," she said, her full cheeks flaming in the light of a lamp.

"Is everyone safe?" Zet gasped. "Did the mummy—"

"The mummy is gone," Delilah said.

"Is Hui—" Kat began.

"We're all safe. They're inside." She turned and roared over her shoulder, "I mean it boys, stay inside!"

A clatter could be heard. Footsteps and muffled voices. Something smashed. It sounded like a piece of pottery. The voices went dead still.

Delilah's mouth pursed. "Zet and Kat? I'm going to have to ask you to stay away."

Kat made a choking sound. "We're so sorry! We never should have asked you to help us."

Movement from the rooftop caught Zet's eye. Hui was up there but quickly pulled back. Zet frowned. He couldn't believe Hui would hide from his best friends, no matter what was happening. They'd always faced things together.

Zet's shoulders sagged. "We never meant to drag you into this. My mother's worried about you."

"We'll get through it," Delilah said. "But please, don't come back."

"Ever?" Kat squeaked.

Delilah relented. She was a big woman and used to handling rowdy boys. She swept Kat into a crushing hug and barked, "I'm only protecting my family. You can come back when this is over."

"What if it's never over?" Kat sniffed.

Delilah didn't reply.

Zet found himself reeling with shock. His life was being torn apart piece by piece. First the pottery stall, and now their friends. What next, their very lives?

Back home, Zet paused in front of Bastet, the cat-goddess carved of ebony. She watched him from behind silent eyes.

"I wish Aziza had never come to our stall," Zet whispered. "I'm sorry people called him Jugnose. Oh, everything is such a mess!"

Then, he thought of his father. He pictured that strong, smiling face. *Was he all right?* Merit's warning about the treasury filled his head. But there were other ways to curse a man on a battlefield. A mummy had dark powers.

Zet's heart squeezed in his chest. He touched Bastet's paws. "Is this curse affecting Father, too?"

Bastet continued to stare silently from her alabaster eyes. This ancient goddess of the home had guarded their family for generations. Even though her eyes were made of stone, Zet felt sure he read sympathy in them.

"Keep my father safe, Bastet. Please, keep all of us safe."

CHAPTER 10
AN UNEXPECTED VISIT

It was late when Zet clambered up the ladder to the roof. As his feet hit the top rung, an alarmed gasp rang out. It came from the rooftop's far side. His instincts kicked into high gear when he spotted Kat struggling near the roof's edge.

Someone, or something, was trying to pull her off!

"Kat!" Zet cried, sprinting toward her.

"Hurry," she called. "Help me!"

He was nearly there. From below came a scrabbling sound. Whatever was pulling her off was thrashing around. Hard.

A boy's voice said, "By the gods, Kat, I'm going to fall."

Hui.

Zet raced forward to see his best friend dangling from the ledge. And Hui wasn't exactly the most nimble of the bunch.

"Hold on." Zet grabbed Hui's left hand. Kat pulled Hui's right one.

Together, they yanked him to safety.

Hui brushed himself off and grinned at Zet. "What took you so long?" he said. "I was about to be jackal dust."

Zet gave him a lighthearted punch. "How was I supposed to know you were coming over here?"

"When you were at my house, I made that bird noise."

"Bird noise?" Zet said. "I thought that was your brothers choking each other."

"Hmm, yes. Understandable."

Kat flapped her arms. "Will you quit joking around? What happened with the mummy?"

Hui flopped onto Zet's sleeping pallet. "Just let me catch my breath."

Kat turned sheepish and twisted her braid. "Thanks for coming. Even though now you're cursed because of us. You're the best friend we could ever have."

Hui gave Kat a dopey grin. "I wouldn't leave you guys in the lurch."

Zet laughed. "Lurch! That's funny."

Kat crossed her arms.

"Because mummies lurch," Zet said. "You know, when they walk?"

Kat said. "I got it. Thank you very much."

"Do you want to hear what happened or not?" Hui said.

"Yes," he and Kat said in unison.

"All right, well, I heard this creepy moaning outside our house. And so I opened the front door—"

"The mummy was there?" Zet said.

Hui looked almost sick as he dry swallowed. "Yeah. It pointed at me. It started whispering. This fast, muttering whisper."

"A curse," Kat breathed.

"I wasn't just going to stand there and let some monster curse me. So I slammed the door and ran around inside, looking for something to throw at it. But of course, Mother barred the door before I could do anything. And then—here's where it gets really weird—some lady screamed! From the opposite end of the street. No one could see who she was. She just screamed really loud."

Kat's eyes were wide. "That's what happened in our street! A lady screamed and everyone went to look for her."

"That is so strange," Zet agreed.

"And then, after the mummy left? My neighbors were running all over the place, looking for the screaming woman. But listen to this. I saw someone. Someone I *never* expected to see in my street."

"Who?" Kat said.

"That grouchy fisherman from the river."

This made Zet and Kat draw back in surprise.

"Are you sure?" Zet asked.

"The big, scary one? Who helped us get our raft unstuck?" Kat said.

Hui nodded. "Pretty weird, right?"

"Did you talk to him?" Zet asked.

"No. I was still inside and I doubt he spotted me through the window. But I know it was him. I'd recognize his big nose anywhere."

"This is all so odd." Kat stood and wrapped her arms around her middle. She paced a few steps, shivering.

A breeze pulled at Zet's hair. An idea was forming—one he couldn't quite catch. He frowned, thinking.

Kat spoke up. "Why would that scary fisherman be in your street?"

"Good question," Zet said. He was beginning to think they'd stumbled on a clue. *But to what?* "Maybe we should row downriver tomorrow and ask him."

"Maybe . . ." Kat said, although she didn't seem too fond of the idea.

Zet said. "Could they be connected? The fisherman, the screaming woman, and the mummy?"

Kat's brow furrowed. "It is a pattern." She stopped pacing. "Wait. What if that fisherman isn't a man, but a *ghost*?"

Zet groaned. "No, he's not a ghost."

Hui said, "Thank the gods for that. Who wants to fight a ghost? We already have a mummy on our hands. Yikes."

Kat said, "Then what *are* you saying, Zet?"

"What if this is all part of some big ruse?"

"A ruse? Impossible." Kat glanced at Hui. "Right, Hui? No way is this a trick."

Hui looked from Zet to Kat and back again. "Uh . . ." Hui hated picking sides.

Kat said, "Well? Who do you agree with? Me or Zet?"

"You?" he told Kat.

Zet smacked his forehead. "Only because she's glaring at you."

"Maybe."

Zet said, "The screaming lady that can't be found is a pretty strange coincidence. You have to admit, something weird is going on. Right now, our only lead is the fisherman from the river. Why was he in your street? We have to investigate."

Hui nodded. "Well hey, I'm free tomorrow." For some reason, he didn't sound happy about it.

"Why?"

"A palace messenger came before I left. I've been given the week off."

Kat said, "They must think you're cursed and don't want you bringing bad luck to the royal jewelers' workshop."

Hui nodded, looking glum. Did this mean he'd lost his apprenticeship? Did they honestly mean just the week off? What if it was forever?

"Wow. Bad news travels fast in royal circles." Zet slumped down beside his best friend. "I don't care what Merimose said. We can't just sit around. We have to do something. Fast."

CHAPTER 11
SURPRISE ON THE NILE

The next morning, Zet and Kat asked their mother if they could go boating on the river. She agreed, saying it would take their minds off things. The siblings ate breakfast quickly and headed outside.

Early sun blazed down and Zet welcomed the coolness that rose from the paving stones. On their way to the river, Zet and Kat stopped to purchase a honey-cake, which they carefully wrapped in a clean cloth. Then, they detoured past their closed market stall.

A new pile of abandoned pottery lay before the tent. They sighed in unison.

"We better hide this away," Zet said.

Kat nodded. "Let's hurry. I bet Hui's waiting for us."

When they reached the Nile, the raft was still tied to the tree. Hui, however, was nowhere in sight. So they waited.

After what felt like ages, Kat groaned. "We told mother we'd be back before lunch. If we don't leave soon, we'll never make it down-river and back. Where is he?"

Zet rubbed his short hair. "I don't think he's coming."

Kat's hands went to her hips. Her brows furrowed with indignation. "Of course he's coming!"

"I bet his mother guessed what he was up to. You know he's not allowed to see us."

"Uh oh. I hope she didn't catch him sneaking home last night."

"That would be bad."

Nearby, a duck tipped underwater headfirst. Its tail feathers waggled as it foraged on the bottom. When it popped back up, however, its beak was empty. The duck quacked loudly and flew off.

"Maybe we should scrap this until tomorrow," Zet said.

Kat crossed her arms. "Why?"

"You want to go? *Just us two?*"

Kat said, "I'm not afraid of those river people."

Zet regarded her, thinking of how two days ago she didn't even want to investigate. "You should be."

"We have the honey-cake to give him," Kat said.

They'd come up with the excuse the night before. They'd give the fisherman the cake and say it was a thank you for his help the other day. After, they'd casually ask him what he was doing in Kanup Street.

Zet said, "What about the current? Remember how hard it was to paddle upstream?"

"Yes, I remember. But we already paid for the cake, and we got Mother to agree to let us come out. Who knows if we'll get another chance? The fisherman scares me, but the mummy scares me more. And right now, the fisherman's our only clue." She flexed one arm. "Besides, you know what? I think I'm stronger from carting those mountains of pottery home."

Zet grinned despite himself. "We don't have much time."

Kat said, "Let's go, before I change my mind."

Traveling downstream went quickly. The Nile carried their raft swiftly past Thebe's bustling watersteps. The city sights gave way to high walls. Here and there, buildings and shady homes peeked above them. The banks grew thicker with reeds and trees as the river wound its way along. Bees buzzed lazily in the gentle winds.

"We're almost there," Zet warned. "Look, there's that sandbank. Coming up on the left."

"I see it," Kat said.

This time, they were better prepared. Before casting off, they'd fashioned two anchors out of big rocks. "Get ready to weigh anchor. I don't want to get stuck again."

She lay down her pole. "It's really shallow. Now!"

Together, they tossed the rocks overboard. Great splashes sparkled in the sunlight. The raft came to a halt.

"Perfect positioning," Zet said.

Kat nodded.

They glanced toward the hut.

"Look," Zet said. "There's that ancient-looking block with the hieroglyphics I told you about."

She squinted. "I see two blocks."

She was right. *Had there always been two?* And where had they come from?

Something else was different. Footsteps had beaten a wide track through the overgrowth between the hut and the river. On the ground lay dozens of empty reed baskets. Some baskets floated, half-submerged, along the river's edge.

The mysterious sandbar had grown larger.

Zet and Kat slipped into the water and began wading toward shore.

"Hey!" came an angry shout.

The burly fisherman stood in the hut's doorway. Dirt and sweat covered his bare shoulders. He looked even bigger than Zet remembered.

Zet waved and called out a traditional greeting. "In peace, good sir."

"Get away, you!"

Water rushed past Zet's knees as he stood rooting his feet in the silty river. He plucked up his courage and called out, "We brought you a gift, to thank you for helping us."

"I don't want no gift," he snarled. "Didn't you hear me? Get lost!"

"It's a honey-cake."

"Take your stupid honey-cake and scram! Quit bothering us. Hear me?"

Kat's high voice startled Zet. "How rude! You can't order us away. This is public land."

"She's right," Zet said.

"Oh yeah?" the man snarled, advancing into the water. "Says who?"

Zet stepped back a foot. This had been a crazy idea. The raft was anchored; they'd never get free on time. He and Kat couldn't fight this fisherman!

"We'll call for the medjay," Kat said, raising her chin.

Zet knew by the way she knotted her fingers that she was terrified. But the man couldn't know that. Taking a cue from her, Zet puffed out his chest.

"Yeah!" Zet shouted.

The man's lip curled. "And how are you going to call for them, hey? Not like we're in town."

Kat pointed at the partially hidden wall that lay deeper in the overgrowth. "The Treasury Building is just on the other side of that wall. I scream really loud. Believe me, someone will come."

The man hesitated. His whole face flushed red. The flush spread to his neck. His fists balled at his sides. He looked ready to explode.

Zet pulled Kat back a step. He could sense her preparing to scream.

Then, the man's shoulders sank. His leathery face twisted into an apologetic smile. He spoke in a loud voice. "Look, now kiddies. Our poor daughter's in that hut. We don't got a home right now, and she's dead sick. We don't want any trouble."

Kat hesitated. Zet felt uncertain.

A faint voice called out, "Who are you talking to, father?"

"Don't you worry yourself, little dove," he called. "It's just some passers-by."

From the hut, there came the sound of violent coughing. "They won't try to make us leave, will they, papa?"

"No, kitten, don't you worry." Turning to Zet and Kat, he said, "Look here, I'm worried about my girl. We don't want anyone pushing us out of our home, even if it is only a poor hut. We're moving on soon. We're not lucky, not like you and your fancy royal friend."

Zet's face grew hot. "You knew who she was?" he stammered.

"I got eyes. I've been to a public ceremony or two."

"Why didn't you say anything?" Kat said.

"Didn't want any trouble. And I figured she wanted to be hidden, so I played along."

"Oh," Kat said. "I'm sorry about your daughter. Can we help?"

The coughing came again.

The man grimaced. "No. Some priest came and went. It's up to the gods now. We just want to be left in peace."

"At least accept the cake we brought you," Kat begged as the coughing fit grew louder.

"No. Leave us alone. Just like we left your royal friend alone."

"All right." Zet agreed. With all the commotion, he'd momentarily forgotten why they'd come. "One question," he called.

The fisherman scowled.

"Why were you in Kanup Street last night?" Zet said.

"Kanup Street?" the man spluttered. "I was nowhere near Kanup Street."

"But my friend saw you."

"He saw someone else, boy." The angry red color had returned to his cheeks. "Now let us alone. Get away and leave us poor folk in peace!"

CHAPTER 12

NIGHT FRIGHT!

The sun god, Ra, beat down mercilessly as Zet and Kat rowed upstream. By the time they pulled the raft ashore, they were sweat-soaked.

Zet flopped down beside Kat to catch his breath. Starving, he unwrapped the cake and broke off a thick, sticky piece. "That man was hiding schomething," he said, his mouth full. It tasted delicious.

"What are you talking about?" Kat said. "His daughter is sick."

"Mmm. Maybe," Zet said.

"You heard her coughing."

Zet swallowed a large bite. "He looked weird when I asked about Kanup Street. He looked guilty."

"He wanted to get rid of us, that's all."

"Hui knows he saw him—he's an artist, he notices details, he wouldn't forget a face. I think that man was lying."

"Why would he lie? Even if he was in Kanup Street—what does it matter? A poor fisherman can't have anything to do with the mummy. He's taking care of his daughter."

Zet sat up. "Where was his wife? That woman?"

"Who knows? At market buying vegetables? Anyway it's almost lunchtime. Mother will be watching for us. Let's go."

That night Zet lay awake, unable to shake his suspicions. The fisherman had lied, he felt sure of it.

From the opposite side of the roof, Kat's snores drifted through the darkness. Zet's muscles ached from their hard row up the Nile. He rubbed his arms and yawned, exhausted even as his thoughts jabbered on.

If only he could see that mummy one more time, he'd have a better idea of what they were up against. But then what? Confront it? Beg it to stop? Ask what it wanted?

He only wished he knew where it planned to strike next.

An idea came to him.

Before he could pursue the thought, a familiar, bird-like whistle drifted from the street below. Zet bolted upright. He ran to the roof's edge and peered down.

"Hui?" he whisper-shouted at a shadowy form below.

"Who else?" Hui whispered back. "Come down."

"Hold on."

Zet grabbed his sandals and tossed them over. Then he clambered after them. His fingers and toes found foot holes in the mud-brick wall. He made quick work of it and soon landed beside his best friend.

"What happened to you today?" Zet asked.

"Mother."

"We figured," Zet said.

"Where's Kat?" Hui asked.

"Sleeping. Snoring actually. Anyway, good thing you showed up, I have an idea."

Hui rubbed his palms together. "Really?"

"I think the mummy's planning to strike again—tonight."

Hui's mouth gaped. "Tonight? Where?"

"Come on," Zet said. "I'll tell you while we run."

"What about Kat?" Hui scratched his neck and gazed up at the roof. "She'll be mad we took off without her."

"I'm not climbing back up there," Zet said. "But you can."

Hui hesitated. It was no secret he'd do just about anything for Kat. However, after his near-disaster climbing the other night, he gave a sheepish shrug. "Yeah, forget it. Why would she be mad? Let's go."

Zet and Hui ran through the darkness. Eerie shadows loomed in every doorway. A slip of torn, fluttering linen drifted past, swirling and tumbling. Cool air crawled over Zet's skin.

They reached the broad market square. Without the daytime bustle, the sprawling square looked creepy and forlorn.

Hui said, "You think the mummy is going to haunt your market stall?"

"Shh! Not so loud," Zet said.

Ahead, tents crouched against the earth. A breeze set the nearest one trembling. Its fastenings came loose and a linen panel billowed up into their path, striking them both.

Hui shouted, smacking at it. Zet grabbed the flap and tied it back down.

"This way," he hissed, pulling Hui by the elbow.

Hui leaned in and murmured, "Why are we whispering? You think that's going to stop a mummy from finding us?"

"Good point."

Still, they crept on tiptoe to Zet's pottery stall, glancing frantically this way and that.

"Where should we hide?" Hui said.

Zet pointed to their closed tent. "In there. We'll watch through a gap."

"What if the mummy's in there?" Hui asked and gulped, eying the large enclosure. "You first."

Zet squared his shoulders and slipped inside. He froze as his toe brushed something soft. Squinting, he spotted a pair of doves. They cooed in annoyance, but only shifted a few inches before going back to sleep.

Zet motioned to Hui. "It's safe. Don't step on the birds."

Together, they created a strategic hole to look out. That way they could watch the lanes between the other stalls.

"Now, we wait. Might as well get comfortable. I have a couple of cushions back there. Hold on. I'll get them."

Hui said, "No way. This place gives me the creeps. I'm coming with you."

A few moments later, Zet was still fumbling around in the blackness. Those cushions were back here somewhere. If only he could see.

"Hui, quit bumping into me," Zet said.

"There's no room."

"You could have waited," Zet said.

"Fat chance! Like I want to meet that mummy alone?"

Hui stepped on Zet's foot. Zet grabbed his toe and leaped around, knocking Hui sideways. They landed in a heap on something soft.

"Hey, look at that," Zet said. "Found the cushions. Let's go."

They stumbled back out, sending pots and plates rattling in their wake.

Hui hissed, "Shh!"

Maybe it was his terror or the absurd craziness of their situation, but Zet clapped a hand over his mouth as a snort of laughter escaped.

"This is insane," Hui gasped, cracking up. "I want my mummy. Get it? Mummy?"

"S—stop, that's not even funny," Zet said, holding his belly.

Hui banged into a tent pole. "Ow!"

"Seriously, quit it, I can't stop laughing!"

Finally, they wiped their eyes.

"One question," Hui said.

"What's that?" Zet asked, tossing down his cushion and sitting.

A shaft of moonlight lit Hui's face. "What are we going to do if the mummy shows up?"

"We're going to ask it what it wants."

Hui paled. "I was afraid you'd say that."

CHAPTER 13

IT COMES TO LIFE

The moon god, Khonsu, drifted across the sea of stars above.

In the tent, Zet and Hui had long since fallen silent. The breeze moaned. The air tasted of dust and a strange mishmash of spices. Neighboring stalls creaked and flapped, sending ghoulish shadows tilting across the square.

Hui grabbed Zet's elbow. "There! *Next to the date vendor's stall!*"

"Nope. That's not it." Zet stifled a yawn.

"What time do you think it is?" Hui asked.

"Past midnight."

"It's not coming," Hui said. "It would be here by now."

Zet hated to admit it, but Hui was probably right. This whole idea was a stupid dead end. And he was tired. Really tired. Rowing the raft had taken its toll. He wasn't looking forward to climbing the wall back onto his roof, let alone trek all the way home. He wanted to shut his eyes for a few minutes. Rest.

"Let's stay a few heartbeats longer," he said.

"You could have at least brought a snack."

"I didn't plan this, remember?" Zet shifted on his cushion. The giant vase supporting his shoulders felt solid. His eyes drifted closed. His head tipped back.

When Hui shook him awake, Zet was surprised to find himself lying down.

"Z-z-z-et?" Hui cried.

Zet's mouth felt fuzzy; his eyelids felt like a pair of stones. "Huh?" he asked, wiping drool from the corner of his mouth.

Hui squeezed his arm in a death grip. The boy's fingers were like rigid claws. They dug into Zet's forearm, practically to the bone.

"Yowza!" Zet yelped, instantly awake.

"L-look!" Hui gasped, still squeezing.

Zet tried to shake him off. "Calm down, will you?"

"Calm down? CALM DOWN?"

"What's the problem?" Zet said.

"The p-p-p-problem?"

"Yeah. Are you sick or something?" Zet said.

"O-over there!" Hui stammered.

"Over where—" Zet froze. His gulp was audible.

"Are you seeing what I'm seeing?"

Zet made a barely noticeable nod. His thudding heart sounded like drumbeats in his ears. His whole body went rigid. His eyes nearly popped out of their sockets.

"Zet?" Hui said in a high, pinched voice.

Zet made no reply. He was unable to find his tongue.

The mummy stood less than forty paces away.

And its burnt-black face stared straight at him.

"Run!" Hui tried to scramble to his feet. He tripped over his sandals and landed on his behind.

Hui tried again. He knocked over a stack of cooking pots. They flew left and right. Crashed down with small explosions. Pieces zinged everywhere. A large one landed in Zet's lap. Another struck him on the shoulder.

The shatter brought Zet to his senses. As the sounds died, he blinked and shook his head. Terrified or not, this was what they'd been waiting for, wasn't it?

"Don't move!" Zet hissed at Hui.

"Are you crazy? Let's go!" Hui backed away as the mummy lurched closer.

"No—this is our chance," Zet said.

The mummy paused. It tilted its head. Listening.

"Chance for what?" Hui cried. "To die?"

"To find out why it's haunting us!"

"Good luck with that. I'm out of here!" Hui backed up on all fours. He crouched behind a giant water jug, holding onto it like a shield.

Zet faced the creature of death. It looked awful. Worse than he remembered. The mummy's bandages were tattered and torn. Covered with brown stains and black blotches. And that disturbing burned face . . . It was a thing of nightmares. Nothing at all like the cute cat mummy he'd seen on the royal grounds.

A whisper issued from the mummy's scorched mouth. Fast and low. A hissing, otherworldly sound.

"What do you want?" Zet cried. "What do you want from us?"

The creature's right hand rose. It pointed straight at him.

Terror snaked around Zet's ribs; he could barely breathe.

The mummy's whispering rose to a shout. It went on and on. An awful, rhythmic chant.

Awoahaoh huhshhhhh ooohamamima awoahaoh huhshhhhh

The noise gripped the air. Soon, all around them, everything seemed to be vibrating. A wind rose, swirling dust into the air. And still, the mummy continued its awful chant.

Zet swallowed hard and forced his shaking legs to move. Everything inside him shouted *run!* Unsteadily, he got to his feet. Then he wrapped one arm around the nearest tent pole as though it was a friend. And perhaps, after sheltering his family for generations, this tent was.

"What do you want?" Zet shouted again. "Are you Aziza? Tell me what you want!"

The mummy's keening chant rose to a wail.

Zet could take it no longer. He would stop this now, or die trying.

"Who are you?" he cried, letting go of the pole and running out of the tent. "Tell me!"

He only made it a few steps outside. From the darkness beyond, a snarling animal launched through the air.

The jackal.

It dove at him.

Hui screamed.

Zet leaped clear and rolled beneath the tent's sidewall. Then he crouched behind a shoulder-high wall of dinner plates.

Outside the jackal, reeking of musk, could be heard sniffing and snuffling at the lowered tent flaps.

Voices rose from the market's fringes. People were coming. Lots of them. The shrill blast of a medjay's papyrus whistle shattered the air. Zet heard the slap of dozens of sandals weaving through the distant stalls along the market's outer edges. Weapons clanked. It sounded like both the medjay and the Royal Guards were arriving in full force.

"Who goes there?" shouted a man, his voice growing closer. "Show yourself!"

Zet recognized that voice: the Royal Guard—*Renni*—who'd tried to shoo him away from Aziza's house.

"Show yourself!" Renni shouted again, his voice drifting above the warren-like maze of shuttered stalls. Any moment and the crowd would find their way here.

Zet peeked beneath the flap to see the mummy turn and lurch off.

With a low growl, the jackal bared its teeth. Then it spun, claws scraping the ground, and loped off in its wake.

CHAPTER 14

BEETLE-DUNG AND BREAD-WORMS!

"Quick," Zet said. "Out the back." He ran for it.

Hui followed and ducked under the rear flap.

"Which way?" Hui said.

Zet peeked around the side. The light of dozens of lanterns grew closer, sending shadows growing and shrinking, wavering like living creatures. Men shouted and fanned out across the square. They beat the canvas with sticks and yelled, *show yourself!*

Zet pointed in the opposite direction. "Head for that alley. That's where the mummy went."

He took off at a sprint. Hui charged alongside. Shadows closed around them. Only a wan moon lit their way.

"Forget the mummy," Hui gasped. "Are you crazy? Let's go home."

Zet veered left. "We have to go after it."

"Beetle-dung and bread-worms!" Hui cried, but followed anyway.

They reached the alley. Thebans were pouring out of their homes. Whispering. Clutching one another and heading toward the square.

As for the mummy and the jackal, they were nowhere to be seen.

Zet smacked his forehead. "How could we lose them? We were so close! How did they escape so fast?"

Hui grabbed Zet's arm. "Uh—Zet?"

"Hold on, I'm trying to think."

"Zet?" Hui yanked again.

"Not now—"

"Look! Over there!" Hui cried.

Zet looked. All he saw were more crowds. Swelling like the tide. "Look at what?" he demanded. "Did you see the mummy?"

"No—but I saw—"

"Forget it, later. Right now, we need to figure out how to get higher. We can't let the mummy escape again. Quick, this way." Zet dragged Hui down a narrow alley. A dozen enormous baskets filled the far end. Zet tried to pull one out. "Help me. Let's drag it over to that door. The one with the big lintel-overhang on top."

Hui latched onto the basket. "*Pee-ew!*" He clamped his nose shut with his thumb and forefinger. "What's in this thing?"

"Trash."

"Smells like a giant dead fish," Hui said.

"I'll turn you into a dead fish if you don't pull harder."

Hui laughed.

Zet fought a rising grin. "Just pull!"

But what a stench! His eyes were practically bugging out.

"Hey, what's a dead fish good for?" Hui said.

"What?"

"Scaling a wall! Get it? Because fish have scales?"

Zet laughed as he clambered up onto the sturdy basket, pulled himself onto the lintel, and then climbed the rest of the way to the roof. With a bit more effort, Hui scaled up after him.

They reached a small terrace. It was empty. They crossed to the far side and climbed over the partition onto the neighboring terrace. Everyone was down in the street. The boys kept going.

Finally, they reached the tallest house. It stood a story higher than those around it.

Below, the town of Thebes spread out around them.

The moon colored everything a sickly shade of gray. In the distance, mist rose from the Nile in eerie swirls. Fog pooled over its banks, sending thin wisps twisting up the adjacent streets.

And then Zet saw it.

The mummy.

It was moving at a fast pace. Mist curled around its legs. It looked as though it was floating. Flying even. Zooming along at a rapid speed. And it was headed for the edge of town.

"There!" Zet cried, pointing. "Let's go."

Hui groaned. "Look how far that is."

"We'll make it."

"It will be gone before we get there," Hui said.

"Not if we're fast." Zet crossed another three rooftops with Hui on his heels. "Besides, I have a feeling I know where it's going."

"How?" Hui demanded, stopping to catch his breath.

"Look at the path it's on. You know where that leads, don't you?"

Hui frowned. Then his brows flew up.

"No," Hui gasped. "*Noooo!* Not there!"

"Makes sense, doesn't it?" Zet tried to shove his friend forward. "Move."

Hui clutched his head and moaned. "We're dead."

"Hurry!"

"My life is over. And my mother's baking date buns tomorrow. Now I'll never get any."

Zet rolled his eyes. "They'd taste even better if you were a hero. Right? And just think of Kat's face, she's going to be so surprised. I can't wait to see that."

Hui pursed his lips. "Valid point." He motioned Zet forward. "Don't just stand around, lead on!"

Soon they were tearing ahead, legs moving at top speed across the rooftops. They caught a last glimpse of the mummy from their high vantage point. Then the rooftops ended. The boys dropped into the street. Mist swirled around their legs. The air grew briny with the Nile's scent. They kept running.

Buildings began to thin out. Palm trees stretched skyward, swaying like shaggy-headed giants.

They reached the Nile's shore. Out on its misty surface, they spotted an ancient-looking boat. And at the boat's helm, shining brightly in the moonlight, stood the mummy.

"Where's it going?" Hui said.

"It's crossing to the West Bank, the Nile's eternal side. That's where mummies are buried and become immortal."

Hui groaned. "Back to its tomb?"

"It must be. Let's get to our raft, it's close," Zet gasped.

Sure enough, their little raft lay safely where Zet and Kat had left it. The boys jumped on. They paddled into the moving current but the fog was growing thicker. Soon, they saw only misty whiteness in every direction. Sailing blind, they smashed into the far bank.

Together, they secured the raft.

Here the ground was dry and rocky. A rough road led up the sloping hillside. They darted up it. Stones scattered underfoot. Soon they reached a pair of iron gates.

"This is it," Zet whispered.

"Are we really going in there?"

Zet nodded, mouth dry. On the far side, shadowy tombs and statues rose from the ground. The boys eyed the famous graveyard: home of the mastabas, or burial chambers, of Egypt's powerful and wealthy citizens.

The Theban Necropolis.

Fear tickled Zet's scalp. Gooseflesh rose along his neck.

"I've never been inside a cemetery," Hui whispered.

"Me neither."

Gripping each other's arms, they pushed through the gate. The hinges creaked. In the distance, someone or something was murmuring. A low, hissing, rhythmic chant.

Awoahaoh huhshhhhh ooohamamima awoahaoh huhshhhhh

The boys stared at each other. Then the gate slammed shut with a bang.

CHAPTER 15

AVENUES OF THE DEAD

The boys stood frozen, hands glued to each other's arms. Finally, the whispering died. A breeze swirled around Zet's ankles. The air in the necropolis felt cold. Avenues of graves climbed the hill before them. There was no mummy in sight.

Zet peeled his fingers from Hui's wrist and gulped.

They snuck forward, both hunched as if trying to become invisible. Something rustled to their left. The boys yelped.

"Just a mouse," Zet breathed.

"This graveyard looks like a creepy town," Hui whispered. "It's all laid out in streets."

"Look." Zet pointed. "Someone left food there, bread and fruit."

"It's all rotten. *Eeeeew.*"

The eerie moon lit the shadowy lanes between the graves. Some were small and simple. Others were marked by statues and steles inscribed with hieroglyphics. The largest were the mastabas, the tombs said to house whole rooms of treasures—objects the deceased might want in the Afterlife: furniture, jewelry, mirrors, vases, incense, jars of rich ointments, beer, and grains, and all manner of things.

Hui pointed at a mastaba. "That one has a door. But it's blocked up."

"Maybe to keep grave robbers out?"

"Yeah. I don't see the mummy, do you?" Hui whispered.

"There!" Zet cried as the mummy lurched past a stone slab in the distance.

The creature quickly melted into the mist.

But Zet had honed in on its position. The mummy wouldn't escape now. Their luck was improving—the jackal was nowhere in sight.

Swallowing his terror, Zet flung himself uphill after the monster. Hui, breathing hard, stayed with him. The air smelled of dirt and decaying flowers. Zet wiped his face. He couldn't rid his nose of the sweet, cloying odor.

"There," Hui cried. "The mummy's tomb!"

Zet followed Hui's outstretched finger.

The stone mastaba looked like all the others—except for one telling detail.

The mastaba's stone door was missing.

Powerful hands had smashed it wide open. Rocks lay crumbled at the gaping entrance. The sleeping chamber of the dead was no longer sealed for eternity like it should have been. Instead, the mummy had broken out of its tomb to walk the earth. It terrorized Zet, his family, and his friends.

The time had come to confront this mummy and put its haunting to an end.

"Zet," Hui whispered, "This is a bad idea!"

The ink-black hole beckoned, gaping like a screaming mouth.

Together, they crept forward until they reached it. Zet's hands shook as he grasped the tomb's broken walls. Jagged stone pressed into his palms. He raised a trembling foot. Held it over the threshold. Took a deep breath.

"Here goes nothing," he whispered.

Then he crossed over.

Into the blackness . . .

"Zet?" Hui whispered.

No answer.

"Zet!?" Hui shouted. "Are you still alive?"

"Shhh, I'm right here! But I can't see anything." His ankle bumped against something white-hot. "Ow!" he cried.

"Zet!?" Hui shouted.

"Stop shouting," Zet whispered. "Something burned me."

"Oh, by the gods, there's no flame, it's evil—it's black fire!" Hui cried.

"It's not. Just get in here, will you? I think I know what this hot thing is."

"Are you crazy?" Hui said.

"Hold on." Zet crouched and felt carefully around. His fingers sensed the warm glow of a small object on the ground. He touched the base, which was cooler, and moved his hands slowly up the sides. It grew hotter the higher he went. "I was right," he called to Hui. "It's a lamp. Someone was in here with a lamp. It's still hot."

"A lamp? Are you sure about that?"

"Positive."

A shuffling sound followed, then Hui banged into Zet.

"Ow. That's weird," Hui said.

"I know. Crouch down. Feel it?"

"Definitely a lamp," Hui said.

"I wonder if there's a flint?" Zet said.

Both boys swept their hands across the floor.

"Found something," Zet said. "I think it's—yes, definitely. A bow drill. Hold on, let me try to light it."

But using the bow drill wasn't easy. Fumbling in the dark, he worked the bow's cord rapidly back and forth. Hui took a turn. They kept working it, grinding the spindle against the wood block beneath it.

"I smell smoke," Hui hissed.

"We've got an ember. Blow on it—gently, gently!" Zet warned.

"I know how to do it." Hui used his breath to encourage the ember. "Touch the wick to the ember, quick."

Zet moved the wick into position. This was the moment of truth.

If the lamp blazed to life, nothing would be hidden. Not even a sleeping mummy. Or worse, a mummy standing over them.

The wick caught.

Zet leaped to his feet as the lamp devoured the darkness.

Everything stood out in hideous relief. Walls covered in hieroglyphics—curses neither Zet nor Hui could read. The gruesome canopic jars that held the mummy's internal organs.

What caught Zet's gaze, though, was the massive sarcophagus.

The ominous coffin lay dead center.

And they were standing right next to it.

CHAPTER 16
THINGS THAT SLITHER IN THE NIGHT

S tanding stock-still in the wavering lamplight, the boys stared at the sarcophagus.

Hui's face was ashen. "Do you think the mummy's crawled back inside it?"

"I—I don't know," Zet said. "Should we look?"

"N-no way," Hui said.

Still, they shuffled forward, shoulder-to-shoulder, elbow-to-elbow, eyes fastened on the ornate coffin. Painted on its lid was the life-sized image of a man.

Was this Aziza? Zet couldn't be sure. Did he have a jugnose? Maybe. His gaze moved to the figure's arms, which were crossed over his chest. The figure's left hand held a golden ankh: the symbol of eternity. The right hand held something more menacing: a curved blade. A sickle.

This was madness.

No one was allowed inside a tomb!

No one, apart from a priest, was ever even permitted to see a sarcophagus. Or a mummy. Not like this. And these wall paintings— they had to be filled with spells and curses. Were all tombs like this inside? Painted from top to bottom with hieroglyphics and detailed pictures? And what was the price of Zet and Hui being there? Would they be cursed for all eternity?

Zet raised the lantern high over the sarcophagus. "Look," he whispered. "The lid! It's not closed all the way."

They leaned in close to study the gap.

A hissing noise began to issue from it.

"Oh n-n-no!" Hui cried. "I d-d-don't like th-this!"

Sweat trickled down Zet's sides and the lamp shook in his hand. The hissing intensified. He was rooted to the spot, unable to move a single step. Unable to run.

"Z-zz-et?" Hui gasped. "What's happening?"

"I can't move!" Zet cried.

"We need to leave," Hui said.

"We need to look inside," Zet managed through dry lips. "You know we do."

He pictured his family still at home, still safe. But for how long? What would the mummy do next?

"Aaargh!" Hui dug his fingers into his hair. "By the gods—the hissing's getting louder!"

His words broke the spell. Zet set down the lamp. He lunged forward and gave the coffin lid a shove. It weighed a ton. He shoved again and the wood groaned. On the third shove, the lid moved, widening the gap.

"Help me," he gasped. "Help me open it."

Hui's eyes were so wide they shone white. The boys placed their hands on the lid. Together, they pushed with all their might.

It began to shift.

Scraping.

Creaking.

Rasping.

Screeeeeeeeeeeeeeeech!

They got it halfway open when Zet hollered, "Stop! Aaaaaahhhh! Stop pushing, stop!"

Dozens, *no hundreds* of slithering snakes erupted through the gap. They swarmed, hissing, out of the coffin. Tongues flicking, cold eyes shining, serpentine bodies stinking. Everywhere. They were everywhere!

"They're on me," Hui shouted. "Get them off! Get them off!"

He stumbled back, arms and legs thrashing as he threw the snakes clear. His foot connected with a canopic jar. The jar toppled sideways and smashed into the one next to it, and then the next, until all four canopic jars crashed open.

But instead of organs spilling out, the contents came alive.

They were beetles.

Scarab beetles.

"AAAAaaaaahhhh!" Zet screamed.

"AAAAaaaaahhhh!" Hui screamed back.

Zet pulled Hui toward the door. "Run! Run for you liiiiife!"

The tomb walls vibrated with hissing and buzzing. Snakes writhed and beetles click-clacked. Horror whiplashed up and down Zet's limbs as bugs surged over his feet and swarmed up his ankles. He kicked out, trying to shake them off.

His foot hit the lamp. It clattered and broke. The tomb went dark.

"I can't see!" Hui screamed.

Zet lunged toward the moonlit gap. "This way!"

The friends leaped out of the broken door. They threw themselves to the ground and rolled, swatting and shouting.

"They're crawling out!" Hui screamed. "They're crawling out! Get up!"

"Gaaaaack!" Zet cried.

They stumbled backward, grabbing at each other for support.

Zet rear-ended into something. Something big and unmoving.

A giant pair of hands clamped down on their shoulders.

Zet glanced sideways and his eyes almost bugged out. The hand holding him firm was enormous. And it was no normal hand. It was the color of charred wood. The color of rot. Swallowing, Zet peered up.

He was staring right into the mummy's gruesome face!

He went cold all over. Then, he screamed with all his might.

CHAPTER 17
WHO DISTURBS MY TOMB?

"*W*ho disturbs my tomb?" the mummy intoned.

Zet and Hui thrashed, trying to free themselves from the monster's grip. Snakes and bugs continued to pour out from the mastaba's broken door. Glittering. Hissing. Clicking.

Louder now, the mummy cried, *"Who dares disturb my tomb?"*

Zet met Hui's frantic eyes. They'd been best friends since forever. Sometimes, they could practically read each other's minds. So when Zet shouted, *"kick*!" Hui knew exactly what he meant.

Zet drove his heel into the creature's shin. Hui did the same. The monster let out a barely audible *Ooof.* Its death-hold loosened, just enough. The boys ducked out of its grasp, ran a few feet and spun around.

Zet stared, mouth slack.

"Muh-muh-mummy!" Hui managed.

Bugs swarmed up its dirty, wrapped limbs. Up its ratty torso. Over its gaunt, grime-stained hands. The monster with its scorched head and charred eyeholes stood stock-still. Nestled deep in the burned folds of face linen lay a pair of terrifying beetle-black eyes. Watching. *Watching!*

Zet and Hui stood frozen in fear.

The mummy raised both arms. Wind shook its bandages. The monster spread its filthy fingers wide. Snakes slithered across the ground, wound up its legs, coiled over its shoulders, fell from its forearms.

The mummy lunged. Snarling, it grabbed both boys and dragged them into the dark, snake-infested mastaba.

They stumbled over the threshold, Zet and Hui yelling and punching. Zet found himself falling sideways and suddenly knew what he had to do. The lamp! He felt the doused lamp's heat before he touched it. Inside, the oil was still scalding hot.

"Hui, duck!" he shouted.

A shaft of moonlight caught the mummy's face. Zet threw the oil and the mummy screamed in agony.

"Run," Zet shouted, throwing himself out the door.

They ran helter-skelter down the avenues of tombs.

Hui's arms and legs pumped furiously as he ran alongside Zet. They leaped over a small statue. Kept going.

"Next time I think up something crazy," Zet gasped, "Tell me to jump off a dock."

"Gladly. Don't stop, it's after us!"

"Get out of this cemetery, hurry," Zet said, putting on more speed.

At the bottom of the hill, they hurled themselves out the gate and kept running until they reached the river. Their raft was still moored next to the Nile.

"Jump on. Paddle!"

Never had they paddled so fast in all their lives.

They reached the opposite shore, but this wasn't over. Who knew what the furious mummy would do next?

"We need to find Merimose," Zet said as they reached shore and tied up the raft with shaking hands.

"I bet he's in the marketplace," Hui said.

Hui was right. Chaos and blazing lanterns filled the market square. It seemed the whole town was awake. Merimose stood on guard with his officers while the Royal Guard questioned frightened bystanders.

"Merimose," Zet gasped, pushing through a knot of people to the big medjay's side. "We followed the mummy. We know where it went."

"Slow down," Merimose growled. "What happened?"

Zet and Hui started talking at once.

Merimose raised a hand. "Stop. Renni needs to hear this." He turned and shouted over his shoulder. "RENNI! Over here. We're in luck. We've got information."

Renni tore himself away from his men and approached, his blade rattling at his side. The head of the Royal Guard frowned at the boys as they stumbled breathlessly through their tale.

"You should have alerted us," he said. "Crossing to the West Bank on your own? What good would that do? Never mind—you'll answer for yourselves later." He made an angry face. "Take us to this tomb."

Zet and Hui led the search party to the river. Boats were gathered up and the small fleet of medjay and Royal Guardsmen crossed the misty Nile. On the far rocky shore, everyone embarked.

"This way," Zet said, leading the charge uphill and into the ancient mortuary.

But when they reached the mastaba, Zet got the shock of his life.

The tomb was empty.

No slithering snakes or clicking beetles. No broken canopic jars. No lamp. Just a heavy, silent sarcophagus with its lid firmly shut.

Even the signs of their struggle had disappeared. Their footprints had been smoothed over. It was all gone.

Renni said, "Where's the tomb? With the snakes?"

"This is it, right here. See, the door is broken open."

A few dried leaves blew across Renni's toes. "A broken door? That's all you have to show me?"

"Well, there were snakes and beetles. And the mummy was right here. We fought it ourselves."

Renni's lips pursed. "Did you, now?"

A couple of his men sniggered.

"You fought the mummy?" Renni sneered.

"I—I don't know where the footprints went. Someone must have gotten rid of them. Swept the ground or something."

"How dare you waste my time," Renni roared. He waved at his gathering. "You had me bring my Royal Guard all this way for nothing?"

"It's not nothing! I'm telling you, the mummy was here."

"I'll have you punished. My men should be in Thebes, not in some god-forsaken cemetery. I'll see you tried in court for your crimes, I'll—"

"Renni," Merimose boomed. "Can I speak to you a moment?"

"Whatever you have to say," Renni snarled, "Spit it out."

Merimose pressed his lips together. Then he blew out a breath. "I can vouch for these boys."

"Can you now?"

"If they say they saw something, they're telling the truth."

Renni said, "This is my investigation, Merimose, not yours. So keep out of it."

Merimose glared. Very slowly, he said, "With all respect—*sir*—if Zet says he saw that mummy, then I suggest you inspect this tomb."

"How dare you. I'll have your medjay-badge for this! I'll—"

Zet found his hands forming fists at his side.

"And another thing," Merimose said. "Since you're obviously unaware–Zet, Hui, and Princess Meritamen are friends. Good friends, in fact. Next time you speak to Pharaoh, I'm sure he'll also be happy to inform you that—" He leaned in close to Renni and spoke into his ear.

"They what?" Renni sputtered.

"It's true," Merimose said, "they helped Pharaoh solve more than one crime. So I think you best drop this talk of punishment. Immediately."

Renni had gone white with rage. He clutched at his head and let out a frustrated yowl. "Fine! Fine, just go. Just leave and we'll forget this ever happened."

"But the tomb," Zet said. "Aren't you going to search it?"

"Of course I'm going to search it!" Renni howled. "Now get off my crime scene. And keep your nose out of my business."

CHAPTER 18

RUNNING FOR HOME

Zet could hardly believe it was still night as he and Hui paddled back across the Nile. It seemed like ages since he'd left home.

One thing was certain: dawn would arrive soon. The sun god, Ra, was nearing the horizon. When his gleaming rays burst across the land, everyone would wake. Including his mother. And Hui's mother.

If they hadn't already.

Despite the need to hurry, an idea broke into his worries and he froze.

"What are you doing?" Hui said. "Keep paddling! I have to get home. My mother's going to kill me!"

"I just thought of something," Zet said.

"Forget thinking. Think later! Paddle."

Zet said, "I should have told Renni to find out if that was Aziza's tomb."

"Not important right now," Hui said. "Focus!"

"Fine." Zet dug his paddle deep. He kept thinking though. He couldn't help it. Questions seemed to pile up, one after the other. Where had the snakes and beetles gone? And their footprints? It hadn't taken that long to alert the authorities and return to the tomb.

"We're here," Hui said. "Jump off."

The boys tied up the raft and sprinted up the bank. They ran through the mist-damp streets. At the Southern Road they split up, wishing each other luck.

Adrenaline surged through Zet as he neared home.

No sign of movement through the window. So far, so good. Silence gripped his street. He clambered up the rough wall to the roof. At the top, he quietly threw one leg over and then the other.

His sheets were exactly as he'd left them.

He squinted toward Kat's sleeping pallet. She was in bed, mouth open, snoring softly. She hadn't even noticed him missing.

Clearly, no one had.

Zet drew a hand across his brow and blew out a relieved sigh. At least something had gone his way. He only hoped Hui was equally lucky.

Instead of climbing under the covers, he crept over to Kat and shook her awake.

"You did *WHAT*?" she shrieked when he told her they'd chased the mummy to the West Bank.

"Shhhhh!" Zet hissed.

"*You did all that without me*?" she wailed.

"Keep your voice down, will you?"

Huffing, she whisper-shouted, "Why didn't you wake me up? This affects me, too, you know!"

"I know." He had to think fast. "Which is why I need your help."

She eyed him indignantly.

"I mean it. Please?"

"What kind of help?" she asked.

"You're smart," Zet said.

She rolled her eyes.

"So help me figure out what happened with that mummy tonight," Zet said. "Because I can't make sense of it, but maybe you can."

Looking slightly mollified, she pulled her knees up and wrapped her arms around them. "Fine. Tell me everything that happened. Slowly this time."

Zet did. He told her how the mummy showed up in front of the pottery stall, and how they chased it through the streets. He described how it escaped across the Nile in a boat lit by a ghostly glow. He told her about the tomb and the still warm lamp, about the snakes and the beetles. And how they'd rushed outside, only to be caught in the mummy's gruesome clutches.

"So it spoke?" Kat asked, winding her braid tightly in one fist. "When it grabbed you?"

"Yes, that's what I said."

She frowned. "Real words?"

"Yes."

"What exactly did it say?" she asked.

"Something like, *who dares disturb my tomb?*"

She toyed with her ear, thinking. "That is so strange. Since before it only whispered mumbo-jumbo."

"You're right. That is strange."

"I guess it wanted to get the message across—in plain words," she said.

"What's weird is, looking back, it's like the mummy wanted us to follow it. Why else did it light up its boat? It was glowing. It could have easily escaped in the dark."

"Maybe it couldn't help being lit up?" Kat said. "Maybe that's what happens when you're a mummy?"

"It wasn't glowing when it came to our house."

"True." She chewed her lip.

"Here's another question—where did the snakes and bugs go? And our footprints? It's all too unbelievable."

They sat in silence, pondering.

Kat shifted, wrapping her covers tighter around her shoulders. "What about before you got to the necropolis? Anything else you remember?"

"No."

"From the marketplace?"

"Nope." Then he bolted upright. "Wait—I totally forgot!"

"What?" Kat said.

"When we ran out of the square! Hui wanted to tell me something. *He saw someone.* But I didn't listen. I was too busy chasing the mummy. Hui seemed really freaked out."

"Who was it? Who did he see?"

"That's the thing," Zet said. "He never got a chance to tell me."

"Could it be a clue?"

"I'm not sure. We need to find out. But that won't be easy since his mother doesn't want us there. We'll have to sneak over."

Zet eyed the dawn breaking across the horizon. From the rooms below, Apu let out a long wail. These past few days, nothing seemed to comfort the once happy baby. Zet and Kat shared a glance, reading one another's thoughts. *Had the mummy cursed Apu?*

Quietly, Kat said, "I'm worried. Where's the mummy going to strike next? First it came here. Then to Hui's. Last night, our stall."

Zet stared out over the adjoining housetops. Crimson light pooled across tiles and balconies, streaked along walls and doors.

"Who's the mummy going to curse next?" Kat said.

"Good question."

Kat walked to the roof's edge. Fisting her hands at her sides, she gazed toward the center of Thebes. A breeze fluttered her dark bangs. "I'm pretty sure I know. And it won't be good."

CHAPTER 19
WHO'S THERE?

Before Kat could tell him her suspicions, a loud hammering came from downstairs. Someone was banging on their front door.

"Who could that be?" Zet wondered aloud.

"I don't know," Kat said. "A visitor? At this hour?"

They bounded down the ladder and headed for the front room. They reached the door at the same time. Zet was about to yank it open but Kat stopped his hand.

"We don't know what's out there," she said.

In a loud voice, Zet said, "Who is it?"

"Geb," came the muffled reply.

Zet and Kat stared at one another. Geb? The spice-vendor from the market? What was he doing here at the crack of dawn?

Their mother appeared, wrapping a linen robe around herself. "Who's out there?"

"It's Geb, the spice vendor," Kat said.

"Well, open the door."

Zet liked Geb. The spice-vendor was a good man and an old family friend. The man stood on the front stoop, his weather-beaten face wearing a worried frown.

Zet said, "Is everything all right?"

"Er—" The small man hesitated and shuffled his fee

"Come in," their mother said.

"I shouldn't." Geb had his woolen wig in his hands. He wrung it like a dishrag. "Just a quick word."

"We'll be more comfortable inside," she said. "Please. Zet and Kat will bring refreshments."

Geb nodded, looking glum, and plopped his wig back on his head. "All right."

Zet and Kat took care of the refreshments as fast as they could, filling a platter with fresh figs and nuts in the kitchen and dashing back to the front room.

Geb was speaking. "I don't like it either, my lady, but you understand, don't you?"

Zet and Kat exchanged a fearful glance. *What had they missed?*

"Yes, I understand," their mother said, yet her face had lost all its color.

"Understand what?" Zet said, his fingers gripping the platter. "Mother? What's going on?"

"Set the fruit down," she said. "I'm sure Geb is hungry."

Geb looked anything but hungry. He looked sick to his stomach.

Kat said, "Why have you come, Geb? Please, tell us."

"It's not easy, children. I see how hard you work. It's . . ." Geb cleared his throat. "It's this mummy business. The vendors are scared."

"Of us?" Kat said.

"I'm afraid the mummy haunted the market last night," Geb said.

Zet flashed back to hiding in his stall, and the chaos with the medjay and the guards and all the villagers showing up in a panic.

Geb said, "The vendors held an emergency pre-dawn meeting. They're worried that your stall's presence offends Aziza and that his curse will spread to them unless something is done."

Kat said, "You make it sound like our stall is a disease."

Geb said, "I know your stall is one of the oldest. Your great-grandfather was one of the market's founders. Your grandpa was a friend to me, and a good man. Your father's a good man, too."

"But . . . ?" Kat said.

Zet said, "We've already shut our stall. We're only taking returns."

Geb licked his dry lips. "I must beg you to remove it."

"Remove our stall?" Kat screeched. "You can't ask that of us!"

"That's crazy," Zet said. "That stall is our life."

Damp spots appeared on Geb's forehead. "I don't like it any more than you do."

Zet's mother said, "We understand. We cannot risk the mummy hurting them because of us."

Geb wrung his woolen wig in his gnarled hands. "I'm sorry. If it were only me, I'd tell you to stay. But I'm an old man with little to lose. Many vendors have families to support. It's nothing against you, they simply can't fight the undead."

Zet could hardly believe this was happening. His world was crumbling. Lose the stall? Shut it down forever? It was their family's history and future. What would they eat? What about the roof over their head? What would their father come home to? Zet had sworn to keep life steady and safe while his father was away. He'd failed completely. And all because of that mummy!

His throat felt thick. He swallowed hard. He didn't want everyone to see the sadness written all over his face. Going to the door, he wiped his eyes on his tunic sleeve.

Geb said, "We vendors have always stood together. When times have been hard, we've stood behind you, as you've stood behind us. This decision was not made easily."

"No, I figured that," Zet murmured, believing him. Even grumpy Salatis, the date-seller, had come to Zet's aid in the past.

"I'll do whatever I can to help until you get back on your feet," Geb said. "I promise."

Kat's face was red. Her eyes brimmed with tears. "Oh Geb, that's kind, but I don't think we'll ever be able to get back on our feet. Without our stall, we'll have lost everything!"

Not on Zet's watch. He refused to let it come to that.

As Geb made to leave, their mother walked him out into the street. They stood murmuring together, but Zet no longer cared what they had to say. This had gone too far. He was furious and frightened all at once.

He had to stop that mummy, no matter what.

Kat sat on a cushion staring blankly at the floor.

"Kat," he said, causing her to start.

She blinked up at him with red-rimmed eyes. "Yes?" she said wearily.

"You said you knew where the mummy would show up next. Where?"

She unfolded herself from the floor and stood. Taking a shaky breath, she said, "I'll tell you. And we'll stop it together."

CHAPTER 20
FUN AND GAMES

A short while later, Zet and Kat paced the roof, talking over what Kat had told him. He was sure she was right. They began to make plans. When the time came, they'd ambush the monster and take him down once and for all. Or be cursed for all eternity. Either way, this had to end.

"Zet, Kat?" their mother called up to them. "Get your sandals on. We're going out."

"Out?" Zet climbed down the ladder.

Their mother wore a simple linen day-dress and Apu was settled on her right hip. The baby chewed fiercely on his wet thumb. "I think we all need a break," she said. "There's been too much stress this past week. So we're going to take a picnic and spend the day in the public gardens."

"A picnic?" Kat clambered downstairs. "*Now?* But everything's falling apart!"

"Which is why we need to pull together as a family. The good news is that Geb has given us two days. If the Royal Guards fail to stop the mummy's haunting, in two days, we'll do as the market vendors ask. So yes, we're going on a picnic. I've packed a basket. Put your sandals on. It's lovely outside."

"But mother—"

"No buts. We're going to enjoy ourselves. We're going to eat and drink and play games. Everything else, we'll forget until tomorrow."

Zet and Kat stared at one another. What choice did they have?

The family trekked through the streets. Zet carried the heavy picnic basket. He longed to tell their mother everything. But it was too risky. What if she forbade him to act? By the gods, who was he supposed to be loyal to? His mother's wishes, or those of his father? And if he left things up to the Royal Guard, would they really solve the mystery? Could he afford to take that chance?

Kat sidled up to him and whispered, "Do you think Hui got caught sneaking home this morning?"

"I dunno. I wish we could tell him we figured out where it's going to strike next."

"*I* figured it out," Kat whispered.

"Yes, fine. Does it really matter? I just wish we could tell him."

"Well, we can't," Kat huffed.

It seemed they both were on edge. At least Apu seemed happier than he had been in weeks. The baby peered around with wide eyes as they left the dusty streets and entered the lush gardens. The air was heavy with the scent of flowers. Birds fluttered from branch to branch, twittering amongst the blooms.

Their mother laid out a big linen blanket.

At first, Zet felt too wound up to relax. Still, he flopped next to Apu.

It was a beautiful day. You wouldn't even know dark events were swirling around them. A leaf spiraled down and landed on Apu's upturned face. Apu squealed, waving his chubby arms. Kat smiled. Zet couldn't help it. He did, too.

"Want to try the fishing net?" Zet asked Kat.

"All right."

With hard work, swift lunges, and a few timely shouts, Zet and Kat managed to catch three big Nile perch. Their mother regaled them with praise. Then she grilled the fish until the fat crackled and popped, the meat turned deep golden, and Zet's stomach rumbled at the delicious scent. They ate perch and crusty bread until their bellies were full to bursting.

When the day cooled and they packed up, it felt like they'd gone on a long holiday.

Yes, there were troubles ahead. But as they walked together in the growing twilight, their eyes shone with happy smiles. They had each other, and that's what was important.

Back home, they once again faced the stacks of returned pottery.

Their mother ran a hand over a large soup-serving dish. "It's lovely, this tureen, isn't it?"

"I remember getting that," Kat said. "On last year's trip to the artisan village."

"Do you remember the boat ride home?" Zet grinned. "When we nearly got overturned by those hippos? Kat, you were screaming and screaming."

Their mother smiled. "We were all screaming."

"You're right," Zet said.

"Especially when that hippo started bellowing." Kat did a mock imitation of a hippo, which sounded more like a cow with a bad case of constipation.

The sound of her snorts and roars soon had Zet and his mother in stitches. They doubled over, laughing until tears ran down their cheeks and they had to beg her to stop.

Apu stuck out his tongue and sent a wet *PLLLFFHHLUT* at them all.

That sent everyone into fresh gales of laughter.

The following day dawned bright and hot. It offered a fresh distraction for the city of Thebes. The Wag Festival of the Dead was drawing near. As part of the celebration, Princess Meritamen's statue would be unveiled at the Temple of Isis. The unveiling would take place that afternoon.

Zet couldn't forget how much Merit dreaded having a statue of her likeness placed in plain sight. Zet didn't blame her, she'd never be able to walk around without being recognized, and she might never get to come out on the raft again or hang out like normal friends.

His own worries about the stall hung heavily on his shoulders: if this haunting didn't end tonight, tomorrow their beloved family stall would be forcibly removed from the market.

At home, no one voice their fears.

From outside came the lively chatter of people in the streets. Busy voices drifted through the open windows. Dressed in their finest, it seemed everyone was headed for the town center.

Kat said, "Mother, are you sure you don't mind us going to the unveiling without you?"

Their mother peered out at the crowds. "Of course not. Princess Meritamen is your friend. You must go. I'm sorry Apu isn't up to it. I think he got a little too much sun yesterday. Come, I'll walk you to the door."

Zet and Kat kissed their mother goodbye and joined the crowds.

They'd barely turned the corner when a figure darted out of an alley and grabbed Kat's elbow.

Kat screeched. Clutching at her chest she said, "Hui! You scared me half to death!"

"Sorry." Hui grinned. "Couldn't let your mother see me. Because she'd tell my mother and I'd be in huge trouble."

"She wouldn't," Zet pointed out, "Because our mothers aren't talking."

"Right. Good point," Hui said.

Kat said, "I heard about you and Zet chasing the mummy."

"Uh oh." Hui glanced at Zet. "Are you mad? I wanted you to come, I swear it!"

"Maybe," she admitted. "But it doesn't matter. Because guess what?"

Cautiously, Hui asked, "What?"

"I figured out where the mummy's going to show up next. And we're going to stop it this time. The three of us."

Hui gulped. "I don't know, Kat . . . you weren't in that cemetery. It was scary." He brushed at his neck as though recalling all those beetles.

"This time will be different," Zet said.

Hui had come to a full stop. "I don't see how."

"Because I have some serious suspicions about that mummy."

"Yeah, that it's going to curse us for good?" Hui asked.

"No, listen, let's cut down this side street. I'll tell you in a minute. After we climb onto that roof," Zet said.

They veered away from the crowds. The Temple of Isis where the unveiling would take place wasn't far now. But Zet, Kat, and Hui weren't going there. Zet and Kat felt certain that the mummy would put in an appearance. Soon.

This very morning, in fact.

In broad daylight.

They needed a good place to watch for its approach. Even more, they needed a spot from where they could track its escape.

"Perfect," Zet said when they'd climbed atop a row house. Like many row houses in Thebes, this house was attached on either side to at least a dozen more. "We can see the Temple of Isis and the whole square from here."

Kat pointed. "Look, there's Pharaoh. And Merit. Up on the Temple steps."

The Princess and her father, dressed in regal garb, shone golden in the light. Jewels glittered in an elaborate necklace at Merit's throat. Pharaoh wore the striped nemes headdress and carried a golden scepter. The royal father and daughter seemed larger than life.

Beside Merit stood a towering object draped in gilt-edged white linen: the statue.

As the square filled to bursting, musicians began to play.

The festivities had begun.

Zet had a bad feeling about this. He only hoped his plan worked.

CHAPTER 21

SHE SCREAMED

From their perch, high on the rooftop, Zet, Kat, and Hui gazed across the crowd at the royal family. It was a glorious day.

Suddenly, Hui grabbed Zet's arm. "Get down!" he gasped, yanking all three away from the roof's edge. "Quick, get down!"

"What's happening?" Kat cried, throwing herself flat.

For a moment, the children lay there, panting.

"Is someone coming?" Zet hissed.

"By the gods, I saw them!" Hui said.

"Saw who?" Kat demanded.

"You know who, from before—oh what if they saw us!"

"Who?"

Hui scooted backward and angled himself behind some potted plants. "Get back here, will you?"

Zet raised his chin and chanced a look around.

Hui grabbed Zet's ankle. "By the beard of Ptah, what are you doing? Are you crazy?"

"Is it the mummy?" Kat said. "Did you see the mummy?"

"Of course not. I told you, it was that person I saw before. *Ohhh!* I hope they didn't see us."

In a fierce whisper, Zet said, "*Who* are you talking about?"

"The other night, like I told you."

"The fisherman?"

"No." Hui peered around the potted planter. "Oh gods, she's still there."

"*She?*" Zet and Kat crouched behind Hui and all three peeked around the big urn.

"Whoa!" Zet said.

A woman stood on a rooftop, not ten houses away. A line of flapping laundry partially hid her from view. Still, Zet would have recognized her anywhere.

"It's the lady from the river," Kat breathed.

Hands on her hips, the fisherwoman studied the crowd with frightening intensity. Maybe she just wanted a good view of the unveiling? Except that she kept scanning left and right as if to confirm she wasn't being watched. It wasn't normal. Something was up.

As if sensing his eyes on her, the fisherwoman swiveled toward Zet.

He hunched down, his thoughts spinning. "So that's who you were trying to warn me about the other night in the marketplace? When we were chasing the mummy?"

Hui nodded. "She was there, in the crowd."

Kat sat down hard. "Why? How?"

Zet said, "So let me get this straight. When the mummy haunted your house, the fisherman was in your street. Then, when the mummy haunted the marketplace, his wife—that fisherwoman—was there?"

"Uh huh."

Kat said, "But this means—"

"They have to be involved," Zet said, cutting in.

Kat frowned. "No. That doesn't make sense. How, by the beard of Ra, could a pair of fisherfolk be involved with a mummy? And what about their sick daughter?"

"I don't think there *is* a sick daughter," Zet said. "We never saw her. I think they made her up."

"*What?*" Kat gasped.

Zet rapidly reviewed the clues in his mind. The man and woman had appeared at every haunting. And there were strange facts about the mummy itself. Why had it been lit up in that boat? Why had it spoken real words in the necropolis? Merimose, their medjay friend, warned that the mummy's touch would turn them to dust. Yet Zet and Hui were both very much alive. He had to think fast, to put all the pieces together while the woman was still nearby. He had a terrible feeling, though, that everything was about to go wrong.

He burst out with a sudden revelation. "That mummy—it was using the lamp we found in the tomb. It must have been!"

Hui said, "I dunno. You think a mummy knows how to use a lamp?"

"And it left the lamp in the tomb for us to find. So that we'd light it and be scared out of our minds. So that we'd go and call the medjay and the Royal Guard."

"Why would the mummy do that? And if that's true, how did it get rid of everything in the tomb?"

Zet grew excited. "Easy. The mummy had help."

"Hah. Very funny. Who would help a mummy? More mummies?" Hui burst out laughing, and then slapped a hand over his mouth. "Wait —there are more mummies? That's what you're saying? Like, an army of mummies? And they're going to take over Thebes? That's why we're up here? I should have known. Oh, this is the worst. The absolute worst."

"There's no army of mummies," Zet said.

"No mummies?" Hui cried out, his face damp.

"Then w-w-what is t-t-THAT? *Over there!*" Kat cried.

She'd raised herself to peek at the Temple of Isis. Her finger shook as she pointed at the temple's rooftop. Zet stared at the mummified figure that was crawling across it on all fours.

Hui said, " By the wings of Isis, they're coming! The mummies are coming!"

"Shush!" Zet said as the mummy reached the temple's roof edge and leaned out over the royal pair below.

"Oh no," Kat gasped. "No!"

The awful sight made Zet's stomach somersault in fear. What was it going to do? He had to warn Merit and Pharaoh. But how? They were too far away!

The crowd hadn't spotted the monster. Their eyes were focused on the statue that was about to be unveiled.

Now, however, the mummy straightened. It angled upright in all its horrifying glory. As it raised both hands, several people pointed. A murmur spread through the crowd. Men, women, and children began to shout and scream. They shoved at each other, trying to flee. The square was so tightly packed that they were trapped.

Princess Meritamen and her father spun to look at the roof. Then Merit and Pharaoh disappeared from view as the Royal Guard closed around them. A protective net of spears and shields formed over their heads.

In the square, the medjay blew their whistles, trying to control the crowd.

On the temple roof, the mummy moved with stiff, jerky motions. It backed out of the crowd's view. Zet, from his vantage point on the roof, however, could see it perfectly. Who would chase the mummy, now that the authorities had their hands full?

The monster lurched into a jerky run. It moved with the speed of a strange acrobat, leaping across the ancient temple's roof.

And then a woman screamed. Her scream tore through air, loud and ringing, making the heaving crowd stop in shock. It was the same high scream Zet had heard that first night when the mummy had roamed his street.

AAAaaaaaaahhhhhhhh!

The bloodcurdling wail sounded like a woman's dying breath.

AAAAAaaaaaaaahhhhhh! AAAAAaaaaaaaahhhhhh!

Despite the chaos on the ground, people searched for the scream's source. The medjay abandoned their crowd control and ran to investigate. Merimose, his eyes fierce, led the chase. Clearly, the big medjay meant to get to the bottom of the mystery screamer.

But Zet now knew the screamer's identity. Everything was falling into place. He had a strong suspicion of what this was all about.

His eyes fastened onto the screaming woman, who stood partially hidden behind the hanging laundry.

"The screamer—" Kat gasped. "It's the lady from the river!"

CHAPTER 22

THE CHASE IS ON!

The three children huddled behind tall vases, staring across at the fisherwoman.

"What does this mean?" Kat whispered.

"Stay down, let's watch where she goes," Zet said.

Hui said, "What about the mummy? It's getting away."

"Oh, shoot—come on, we need to move." On all fours, Zet crawled for the roof's far side. The sun-scorched surface felt hot under his hands and knees.

"Where are we going?" Kat said.

"To the river. Stay down!"

Hui scuttled along on all fours. "The river? You want to go back to that creepy tomb?"

Kat said, "*Zet?* What's going on? Hello!"

"There's no time, just hurry! To the raft!"

Zet wanted to explain, but he was pouring all his energy into running. They crossed several rooftops, and when they reached the shortest house they scrambled onto an awning and dropped to the ground. Except for the pigeons, here the streets were empty. The echoes of market chaos faded behind them as they made for the river.

Finally, they reached the Nile's shore. All three stood with their hands on their knees, bent double, breathing hard. Zet swallowed, his mouth parched.

"We've got to get to that fishing shack," he said.

Kat and Hui reeled in shock.

"The fishing shack?" Kat demanded.

"Something terrible is about to happen. We have to stop it."

"Stop what?" Kat said. "Zet, you're not making any sense. Is the mummy going to attack the fisherfolk?"

Zet smacked his forehead. "By the gods, I just realized something."

"*What?*" Kat and Hui demanded at once.

"One of us has to go for help. We need backup. Someone has to go for the medjay. Or the Royal Guard."

"ZET!" Kat said in a furious voice. "Unless you tell us what's going on right now, no one's going anywhere."

Zet nodded. As quick as he could, he explained. Kat and Hui's eyes grew wider and wider.

"I don't believe it," Kat cried. "This threatens all of Egypt!"

"Not if we stop it," Zet said. "So who wants to go for help?"

Kat said, "Don't look at me. I'm coming with you. This started at our house."

"What?" Hui said, brows flying up. "I'm not going for help! That Renni guy hates me. He'll clap me in chains if I bug him again."

Kat glared at him.

Hui, who hated disagreements, threw up his arms in defeat. "Fine. Fine, I'll go."

"Thank you," Kat said in a tight voice.

Hui puffed out his chest and adjusted his tunic. "But don't forget, this whole thing would fall apart if I hadn't volunteered."

At this, Zet had a horrible sense of foreboding. What if Renni and his Royal Guards wouldn't listen to Hui? But there wasn't time for a better plan.

Hui saluted. "I'm off!"

"Good luck," Zet said.

"You, too."

"See you on the other side," Zet said.

Hui dashed off and disappeared around a corner.

"Let's get the raft in the river," Zet said

The siblings splashed up to their knees in the cool water, pulling their raft. They clambered aboard, poles in hand. The current grabbed hold and they started moving. They traveled the familiar route, too tense to speak.

As they rounded a bend, Zet whispered, "We're almost there. Let's hide the raft."

They pulled it ashore, tucking it into a thicket of undergrowth. A sudden breeze sent tamarisk blooms raining into Zet's face, momentarily blinding him. He brushed them away and crept forward with Kat at his side.

Soon, the fishing shack came into view.

To Zet's surprise, the area was deserted. Baskets lay here and there. Dozens of them. Darting forward, the siblings peeked into the baskets and found them empty.

Kat grabbed Zet's shoulder and pointed. "Look how high the sandbank is!" she whispered. "They've been emptying dirt out there, using the baskets to do it. That's why it got so shallow. They must have been digging for days. And there's a boat!"

A big expensive-looking boat floated at anchor, just beyond the sandbank. The hull was made of wood and its sails were rolled up. The boat could carry dozens of people.

"Seems like no one's on it," Kat whispered.

"Not yet," Zet whispered back. "Let's check out the hut."

Kat swallowed. "All right."

Zet glanced inland to where the wall partially hid the Treasury Building from view. His muscles tensed in fear. Who was guarding the Treasury now?

With a mummy on the loose, all of Thebes was in chaos. Was it possible the Royal Guard had been forced to abandon the Treasury in order to protect the royal family?

Zet feared the worst.

He nodded at Kat. "Let's go."

CHAPTER 23

THROUGH THE DOOR

Together, the siblings approached the wooden hut. A breeze moaned in the treetops and whispered through the grasses. Zet's wet sandals made squelching noises. He slipped them off.

"What if someone's in there?" Kat whispered.

"*Shhh!*" he cautioned and slowly pushed open the door. Just a crack.

Carefully, he squinted into the gloom.

"Empty," he whispered.

At his elbow, Kat gulped loudly.

They inched inside. Shafts of light stabbed through the rough-hewn walls. The place stank of sweat and old food. His foot squished down on something spongy. A moldy loaf of bread. *Eeew.* Gingerly, he kicked it away. Dirty sleeping pallets lay here and there. At least a dozen of them. The shack was bigger inside than it looked from outside, stretching backward away from the river.

Kat wrinkled her nose. "Someone needs a bath," she whispered. "Bad."

"Whoa, take a look at that!" Zet pointed at a massive gap dug into the earth. He covered his nose, hopped over reed mattresses and bee-lined for the dark hole.

"Stay quiet," Kat warned.

"I was right. *A tunnel!*"

That's where the sandbank came from. The fisherfolk had clearly been digging for days. They'd been carrying dirt out in baskets and dumping the dirt in the river. No wonder the raft had gotten stuck.

Zet thought of Hui. *Please let him bring the medjay and the Royal Guards. Fast!*

"I wish we'd brought a lamp," Kat whispered as they made their way into the tunnel.

"It's better we didn't."

"I can't see."

"Use your hands, feel your way," Zet said, dragging his fingers against the cool earthen wall as they shuffled deeper into the blackness.

At least the dirt was hard-packed, but was it enough to make the roof stable? What if the ceiling tumbled down and buried them deep underground? He tried not to shudder at his fear of being entombed alive.

His fingers touched what felt like a wooden beam pressed into the wall. He stopped to trace it in the dark. The beam seemed to connect with another slat overhead. A support arch. Clearly, the diggers had put a lot of work into this tunnel.

"How much further?" Kat whispered.

"I think I see a light ahead."

A glow flickered in the distance. It grew brighter as they drew near. Zet realized he no longer needed to use the wall to find his way. This was it. Any moment, he'd know if his suspicions were correct. Part of him wished desperately to be wrong. His heart thumped in his ears and he wondered if he'd ever again see the light of day.

Zet's knee slammed into something warm and solid. He tripped and fell flat on his face. Something thrashed and moaned under him.

"Zet?" Kat hissed. "There's someone here!"

Zet squinted in the half-light. He saw a man, bound and gagged. The man wore a gilded headdress and a robe of fine linen.

"He's tied up," Zet whispered. "Help me."

Kat got down beside Zet. But they had nothing to cut the ropes. Zet pulled the gag from the man's mouth. The man sighed in relief.

Kat whispered, "Who are you?"

"My name is Ptahmose. I'm the Overseer of the Treasury."

Zet nodded. He expected as much. "Are you all right, sir?"

"Yes. Thank you. But you mustn't worry about me. Go back the way you came, and bring help!"

"The authorities are already on their way," Zet said, hoping it was true.

Until then, though, they needed a way to prevent the evil intruders from escaping.

An idea came to him. "We'll have to cave in that tunnel-section up ahead."

"But the Treasury!" Ptahmose said.

"It's the only way to stop this," Zet said.

"Then go with my blessing."

"I just wish we had some tools to jab at the ceiling," Zet said.

"Then you must get into the Treasury. You'll find swords and spears and all manner of things if you can get inside without being seen," Ptahmose said. "And be careful the ceiling doesn't fall on you."

"We'll do our best."

Ptahmose nodded. "May the Gods be with you."

As Zet and Kat closed the final distance, Zet's heart hammered so hard he felt dizzy. Beside him, Kat was shaking. The increasing light was soon accompanied by chaotic sounds—clanking and shuffling, grunts and the rasp of heavy objects being dragged across a stone floor.

And then they arrived.

The tunnel mouth opened into a vast bright chamber.

Everything seemed to be glittering. Mounds of golden objects. Reams of spun fabric. Goblets and jewel-encrusted platters. Ceremonial daggers and breastplates. Trunks with their lids thrown open to reveal necklaces, rings, bracelets, and turquoise-studded amulets. There were objects from foreign lands—things that mystified Zet beyond all understanding.

He sucked in his breath. Kat did the same as they crouched in the tunnel's shadow and peeked out.

But it was clear that the Royal trove was only a fraction of what it had once been. The Treasury was nowhere near full. Princess Merit had been right. Worse, the remains were now disappearing into the hands of plundering thieves.

Lining each wall, stone-faced statues of long-dead pharaohs looked helplessly down at the awful scene unfolding. Eight men and two women shoveled plunder into sturdy sacks. Three more hulking men dragged the bags across the floor with filthy hands and heaved their booty into waiting carts.

Thirteen powerful, cunning thieves in all.

And they were just two children.

Zet swallowed hard, eyes searching for the weapons that the Overseer had mentioned. After a moment, he located a stand bristling with metal-tipped spears.

Could he possibly grab a spear and run back without being spotted? Would he be able to jab at the ceiling fast enough to bring down a section and trap the thieves inside? It seemed an impossible task. A stupid one, even. But what other plan did they have?

If only help would arrive!

He shot a hopeful glance toward the Treasury's colossal pair of front doors. Dust motes swirled in the vast space between them. How he wished those giant doors would fly open with Hui leading the charge.

But the Treasury doors stayed firmly shut. It was probably still chaos back at the statue unveiling. Merimose, Renni, and their men had their hands full protecting Merit and Pharaoh. The whole city had witnessed the mummy's gruesome visit. A vengeful creature from the dead. It was the only emergency for which the Treasury guards would abandon their post and rush to protect Pharaoh at all costs.

Days ago on the raft, Merit had said it would be impossible to bust down the Treasury entrance. But the thieves hadn't come through the front doors.

He turned to Kat and placed a finger to his lips. *"Wait here,"* he mouthed.

She looked white as a sheet, but ready to join him in a dash for the spears. He shook his head sharply, making silent gestures to argue that one person would be less conspicuous. Brows knitted with worry, she gave a frustrated, frantic nod.

Adrenaline ripped through him as he tiptoed out into the open. Every nerve stood at attention as he padded toward the stand of javelins.

A man grunted and the sound ricocheted through Zet with the force of a blow. He faltered and glanced right. A thug with lank greasy hair was tossing heavy bags into a narrow cart. He hadn't spotted Zet.

The stand of spears was so close. No more than a few feet. Almost there. He couldn't stop now. Except the thug was straightening. The thief lifted the cart handles and angled it toward the tunnel entrance. The wheels began to creak.

Zet closed the last few steps, pulled a spear free, and broke into a run.

"Hey!" the thug roared.

If Zet so much as stumbled, he was toast.

He reached the entrance and saw with relief that Kat was gone. But then he nearly stumbled over Ptahmose. Kat was on her knees beside the Overseer. She'd found a dagger and was trying to slice through his ropes. Suddenly the man's hands were free.

"They're coming!" Zet gasped, pulling his sister to her feet. "There's no time to bring the roof down. We have to scuttle their boat. Quick, it's the only way!"

"Go," the Overseer said, grabbing the dagger and sawing the bonds at his ankles. "It's up to you to save Egypt's treasures!"

CHAPTER 24
THE MOUTHS OF CROCODILES

Zet and Kat ran. The tunnel soon swallowed them in darkness.

With a jolt, Zet's speartip caught against the low roof. He staggered to a halt, nearly thrown by the impact.

Kat charged ahead, panting in the darkness.

From behind, the thugs roared with savage shouts that echoed along the passage. Zet yanked on the spear. It was stuck fast. He abandoned the weapon and pelted after Kat.

Ahead, the tunnel grew brighter. He could smell the dank shack before they reached it. They tumbled out of the passage, leaped across the mattresses, and burst through the door into the bright sunlight. They left the door flapping and ran for the boat.

Water splashed as they half-swam, half-dove to the bobbing vessel. The siblings scrambled up the side, using the anchor rope as leverage. When Zet's feet hit the deck, he heard a strangled shout.

Kat screamed and pointed. "The mummy! It's after us!"

She was right.

The mummy, its evil wrappings filthy and tattered, loped across the sand. It closed the distance, fast, the jackal on its heels.

"It's coming, pull up anchor!" Kat screamed.

Too late.

The mummy reached the vessel's side. Its dirt-blackened hands took hold of a rope, and beetle-black eyes glared from between the bandages. The siblings watched in horror as it hauled itself aboard. The deck creaked as the creature lurched toward them.

On the riverbank, the jackal pranced this way and that, snarling and gnashing its teeth.

Zet spun, searching for a weapon and finding none. The foul odor of rotting linen assaulted his nostrils as the mummy tackled him. The powerful monster threw Zet to the ground. Locked in a death-grip, they rolled across the deck.

Kat danced around them, screaming and kicking the mummy and trying to haul it off.

"The anchor!" Zet gasped, as powerful hands pinned him in place. "Pull up the anchor! We have to get away from shore before the thieves get here!"

Kat knew he was right, for she sped away.

An awful laugh bubbled up from the mummy's throat. Its glittering eyes glared, hard and cold. The deck lurched sideways. Together, the two of them slammed up against a railing. Zet drove his knee into the mummy's midsection.

It was a perfect shot. The mummy let out an angry shriek.

Zet rolled clear and leapt to his feet but the mummy was up, too. It pounced again. Zet tried to block and his fingers caught in the rotting bandages. As he jumped backward, the bandages came with him. They were unraveling.

The mummy roared.

Horrified and fascinated, Zet started to pull.

A dozen paces away, Kat struggled with the heavy anchor. She hauled it partway out of the water and the boat started floating downriver, fast. But she lost her grip and the anchor splashed into the Nile. A hard jolt sent Zet, Kat, and the mummy sprawling to the deck. They'd come to a full stop.

"Argh," the mummy groaned, rising and tottering away.

Zet ran after the mummy, grabbed a trailing bandage again, and pulled. As he did, the mummy began to unwind.

"Help me," Zet shouted.

Kat ran to his side and grabbed hold. They tugged, hauling at the long, grimy strip. Howling in shock, the mummy began to twirl and twirl. Faster and faster. The bare skin of one hand appeared. Then came a dirt-smudged arm. Followed by a bony shoulder.

Zet and Kat shared a startled look and kept pulling.

This was crazy!

Around and around the mummy spun until it was no longer a mummy but a tall bony man dressed in his loincloth undergarments. Finally, the last of the wrappings came free, except for the blackened bandages covering his face. The man kept spinning a few more times before he plonked onto his behind with a hard thump. Moaning, the man grabbed his head.

"Who are you?" Zet demanded, trying to pull the off the burned-black mask. "You're not a mummy! Who are you?"

But just then, on shore, the thieves burst out of the shack. The huge fisherman was in the lead.

"Stop those kids!" snarled the fisherman.

Zet and Kat shared a terrified glance. They'd never be able to pull the anchor up on time to sail out of reach. They needed to do something, but what?

"Those barrels," Kat gasped, pointing. "Are they food barrels?"

Zet knew exactly what she was thinking.

"Come on," Zet said. "Hurry!"

"Dried fish," Kat cried as she tore off a barrel lid.

"Perfect," Zet said.

Together, they tossed stinky fish hunks overboard. It took mere moments for the first crocodile to appear. Huge and brown, its leathery snout looked as long as Zet's whole body. Hungrily, it snapped up the first mouthful.

The thieves, who had plunged into the river, scrambled backward.

A second crocodile rose up, ancient-looking and knobby-headed. And then a third. The water churned with monsters.

The thugs screamed and retreated to shore.

From behind Zet and Kat came an enraged shout. The mummy-man was on his feet and they watched in horror as he peeled off his gruesome mask. It came away in sticky strips. Underneath, thick black smears of kohl lined the man's eyes. Now Zet understood: the kohl, grease, and singed mask is how he'd created his burned look!

Zet's stomach dropped. "You!" he cried.

"Yes, me," the man said.

It was the *Royal Mummifier!* The man who had once leered at Zet and Merit through a jackal's mask. No wonder he'd seemed suspicious that night when Zet had tried to question him about Aziza.

"But you're the Royal Mummifier!" Zet cried. "How could you do this?"

"How? I am gifted with the power of the gods. I will be rewarded with the gold and riches I deserve. And I will destroy you children for trying to ruin my plans!"

He dashed forward, reaching his bony hands for their throats. The boat, however, rocked unsteadily. The children leapt clear and the Mummifier sprawled to his knees.

At that moment, on shore, Hui came flying out of the shack.

Merimose was on his heels.

Behind Merimose came Renni.

And behind Renni came the whole of the Royal Guard and countless armed medjay police.

"Stop, you up there, whoever you are!" Renni shouted, pointing at the grimy-faced Royal Mummifier. "You're under arrest."

Zet and Kat cheered and whooped. On shore, Hui did the same.

"You've ruined everything!" the Mummifier screamed at Zet and Kat. "The gods will punish you for this!"

"Somehow, I doubt that," Zet said.

"Yeah," Kat said. "I don't think the gods are going to be too happy with you after this."

"You know nothing of the ancient religions. I alone know the secrets of the dead," the Mummifier said. Then he shook his fist at the gathered fishermen. "You fools! I should have never trusted you idiots to carry out my plan."

The big, burly fisherman shouted back. "You stupid cretin, you never should've talked to these dumb kids in your fancy temple. It's all your fault!"

The continued to shout insults back and forth, but Zet ignored them. Instead, he gave the bandages another tug and the Mummifier tripped, falling flat on his face. Zet and Kat dove onto his back and tied his wrists with the linen strips.

Then Zet glanced over the boat's side to see Merimose grinning broadly and rounding up thieves. The jackal, which turned out to be a huge dog, was tied to a tree. A medjay tossed the dog a bone and it flopped down to chomp away in silence.

The shack's door opened once again and the Overseer of the Treasury limped outside. His gold-trimmed robe was torn and his cheeks were grubby, but his face was lit up. He waved at Zet and Kat.

"Well done!" he shouted. "Well done, my young friends!"

It took ages for the hungry crocodiles to leave. When it was safe, Renni climbed on deck and tightened the Mummifier's bandages.

The priest said, "Let go of me. Or I'll make sure you're doomed for all eternity."

Renni shook his head. "I'm sure Pharaoh, the living god, will have something to say about that." He sent him over the side into the arms of a Royal Guard.

Zet and Kat jumped overboard and ran to Hui. The three friends whooped and cheered all over again.

Renni approached, curling his lip. "You reckless kids! You should have informed us about this place."

Hui looked offended. "Uh, excuse me, sir? I did inform you!"

With a howl, Renni said, "I meant *before* these two fools rushed down here!"

"Fools?" Kat demanded, her hands on her hips.

"They would have gotten away," Zet said. "They had a boat. They were robbing the Treasury and no one was here to stop them. Except us."

"Yes, well—"

Hui said, "I had to beg you to come. You didn't believe me. You were still mad that we dragged you to that old tomb on the West Bank."

Zet said, "We tried to tell you something was off up at the tomb. But you wouldn't listen. And then we only just figured out that this mummy business was all a ruse. They were doing it to throw Thebes into chaos and get you off the scent! That way the fisherman and his thugs could rob the place. And they almost did."

"Yeah," Kat said. "They got the Royal Guard to abandon the Treasury Building. They had it all to themselves, with a getaway ship waiting."

Zet said, "You were down in the square, thinking you had to protect Pharaoh and Princess Meritamen. While the thieves were inside, filling carts with loot."

Renni's face turned boiling red, whether with rage or embarrassment or both.

Merimose appeared and said, "All right, all right. Let's all calm down here. It's over."

Renni said, "Not until I say it's over. Merimose, haul away those thieves."

"Gladly." Merimose grinned. "After I congratulate Zet, Kat, and Hui for saving the day."

Ignoring the fact that Renni's head was practically smoking with outrage, Merimose bent to thank the children. One-by-one, he shook their hands in his huge leathery grip. Zet laughed with relief as Merimose clapped him on the back.

It was over. It was really over. They'd saved the Treasury funds. There was no evil threat hanging over their heads. No mummy's curse after all.

They were free.

CHAPTER 25

A FESTIVE CELEBRATION

The long shadows of dusk cooled the air as the three children ran for home. Zet and Kat said goodbye to Hui and finally turned into their own street. When they reached their front steps and threw open the door, they heard something wonderful.

Apu was laughing.

Their baby brother, who'd been so unhappy of late, was giggling and chortling.

"Zet, Kat!" their mother cried and wrapped them in a hug. "The news is all over town. I'm so proud of you."

Zet and Kat hugged her back.

From a blanket on the floor, baby Apu called out to them in the best way he knew how. He stuck out his tongue, went *PLLLFFHHLUT.*

Zet swung Apu up. "Hello, baby brother."

"He has something to show you," their mother said. "Right, Apu?"

Recognizing his name, Apu flapped his chubby arms and smiled. And there, poking out of his little pink gums, was a tooth.

Kat's jaw dropped. "Is that why he's been so upset?"

"Yes, poor thing." Their mother stroked Apu's head. "Like I said, growing pains."

Kat flushed. "Oh! And here I thought—"

"You thought what?"

Kat shared a glance with Zet, who recalled how they both thought the mummy had cursed Apu. It seemed ridiculous now.

With a grin, Kat waved her hand. "Oh, never mind."

For the next two days, the house was alive with visitors. Neighbors had come to chat. Customers came bearing gifts of incense, food, cloth, and more. Zet, Kat, and their mother helped their guilt-ridden clients find their beloved dishes, pots, and plates in the stacks that filled the front room. Everyone agreed it had only been natural to fear the mummy's curse. No one bore a grudge.

Hui's mother, Delilah, baked cakes with their mother, which they served to everyone stopping by.

It was late afternoon when Zet, Kat, and Hui snuck away to the roof.

Hui flapped at a fly. "I still don't get why the Mummifier targeted you."

"Easy," Zet said. "He knew we'd make the perfect foil to distract the whole town. Everyone in Thebes knew about that Jugnose business, and that Aziza never forgave us."

"I bet the Mummifier was pretty surprised the night you showed up at his workshop!" Hui said with a laugh.

"Can you imagine?" Kat said.

"He hid it pretty well," Zet said. "But he did seem kind of fishy."

Kat placed another fold in the paper boat she was making for the Wag Festival of the Dead. Everyone in Thebes would be doing the same thing: preparing tiny paper boats to launch on the Nile to honor those who'd passed into the afterlife.

"I guess the Gods were looking out for us," she said.

Zet thought about the desperate prayer he'd made to Bastet days earlier, and how the ebony Cat Goddess statue had studied him with her silent eyes.

Hui frowned. "But what about in the cemetery? The mummy's horrible black face and hands?"

"Lamp soot, grease, and khol," Zet said.

"He sure fooled me," Hui said.

Kat held up her paper boat. "What do you think?"

"Impressive," Hui told her. "That'll be the best one there!"

Kat grinned.

His sister was holding her boat the next day as they stood on a set of freshly polished watersteps next to the Nile. Zet and Hui had boats, too, and so did Princess Meritamen, who stood at their sides.

The Mummifier's ears must have been buzzing, for they'd spent the last twenty minutes talking about him until there was nothing left to say.

"I'm just grateful to have such smart friends." Merit looked nothing like the girl who'd snuck over the palace wall and paddled downriver on a handmade raft. But although she shone with gold and turquoise, Merit had the same laugh and dancing eyes. "And Egypt is grateful, too. You three are heroes."

This left Zet, Kat, and Hui blushing.

Up and down the Nile, citizens of Thebes lined the waterway, crowding as far as they could see. Everyone held their paper boats, waiting for Pharaoh's signal to launch them. Zet, Kat, Hui, and their families stood under the shade of the Royal tent. They were excited to be right at the center of the whole festival.

Merit said, "I have a surprise for you. Well, actually, it was my father's idea."

"A surprise?" Zet said.

Just then, Pharaoh emerged from the royal tent. The crowds along the Nile fell silent, awed by his glittering presence. Pharaoh's face was deeply lined, but his shoulders were still broad and powerful, strong enough to bear the weight of the world.

Pharaoh nodded solemnly at Zet, Kat, Hui, and his daughter.

"If I'm not mistaken," Pharaoh said in his low rumbling voice, "It should be here at any moment."

At that second, the crowd parted to allow a breathless runner through. He was deeply tanned, glowing with sweat, and dressed in a light kilt and sandals. A royal messenger. And it was clear he'd come far.

Instead of approaching Pharaoh, the messenger knelt before Zet, Kat, and Hui. In his hands, he held two scrolls—one for each family.

"Where did you run from?" Kat asked.

"Open the letter."

Kat, who possessed the rare ability to read hieroglyphics, unrolled the scroll and gasped.

She looked at Merit and Pharaoh. "It's from our father!"

Merit said, "We sent a runner north and back because I know how awful it is to worry about your family."

Zet and his mother crowded close, with Apu in her arms.

"What does it say?" Zet said.

Kat's breath caught on a happy sob. "Father's safe. He knows we saved the Treasury. He says, *I always knew I could count on you. I'm so proud of you both. Give your mother and baby brother a kiss for me. I miss you very much. Your loving father.*"

Kat brushed away a tear and their mother did the same. Zet swallowed hard, doing his best not to choke up. Hui, who'd received a letter from his father, was all choked up.

It was a happy day for all.

Music began to play as Pharaoh, the Living God, stepped down to the water's edge. He knelt and spoke quietly as he placed a small paper boat on the Nile's surface. Zet wondered to whom Pharaoh had dedicated his Wag Festival boat. A relative that had gone on to the Afterlife, perhaps?

All along the Nile, a cheer went up. The water soon filled with gleaming white paper boats.

Kat, Merit, Hui, and Zet all knelt together to launch theirs.

"I know who I'm dedicating mine to," Kat announced. "Someone who I really want to be happy in the Afterlife."

"Who?" the others demanded.

"Aziza."

Hui laughed and said, "Good idea."

Merit said, "I'm going to do the same."

Zet said, "Me too." Then he grinned. "Just in case. *Live well in the Afterlife, Aziza.*"

The boat bobbed on the water. He gave it a little push and set it free.

10 Fast Facts About Mummies

1. Egyptians started making mummies over 5,000 years ago.
2. In ancient Egypt, anyone could be mummified when they died, as long as they could afford it.
3. If you unrolled a mummy in one strip, the strip would be 10 football fields long.
4. Embalmers used tree resin or sap to make the linen strips stick together.
5. Without their wrappings, most mummies weigh only 5 pounds.
6. No mummy has ever been found inside a pyramid—they've only been found inside hidden tombs.
7. The mummy of Pharaoh Ramses II once received a passport to visit France.
8. Egyptians chose to get mummified because they believed they could use their preserved bodies in the afterlife.
9. Cleopatra's mummy has never been found.
10. Some mummy curses, including a handful associated with King Tut's tomb, have never been solved.

A mummified cat

Acknowledgments

My thanks goes out to Peter and Judy Wyshynski, to my sisters Jill and Sarah, to Scott Lisetor, Sharon Brown, Amanda Budde-Sung, Ellie Crowe, and Adria Estribou. And to everyone who had a hand in this novel, and who helped me along the way, I say thank you from the bottom of my heart.

Visit Scott's ancient Egypt Website
For activities and facts: kidsancientegypt.com

FREE Reading Comprehension Activity
Get this book's free activity here:
bit.ly/zet-mummy

Bestselling author Scott Peters has created over 300 museum, science center, and amusement park experiences for places such as Disney World, Universal Studios, and the Smithsonian.

Find Scott Peters on Facebook, Pinterest, BookBub and more.

facebook.com/ScottPetersBooks
twitter.com/AuthScottPeters
pinterest.com/AuthScottPeters
bookbub.com/authors/scott-peters
amazon.com/author/egypt

GO BACK TO WHERE IT ALL BEGAN

Go back to where it all began in:

Mystery of the Egyptian Scroll

Or solve a spooky theft with Zet and Kat in:

Mystery of the Egyptian Amulet

DID YOU ENJOY MYSTERY OF THE EGYPTIAN MUMMY?

WOULD YOU...REVIEW?

Online reviews are crucial for indie authors like me. They help bring credibility and make books more discoverable by new readers. I'd love for you to take a few moments and write a short honest review on Amazon and tell a friend about my books.

Join My Readers List!

Get an email whenever I release a new book and receive a free 3-pack of printable, custom ancient Egypt mazes.

Sign up at: http://www.subscribepage.com/scottpeters

CPSIA information can be obtained
at www.ICGtesting.com
Printed in the USA
BVHW040215100423
662047BV00010B/42